MW01248484

1-27-03

Willard Stoltz

Comanche Captive

By Willard Stoelting

Copyright © 2003 by Willard Stoelting

ISBN 0-7414-1393-0

Published by:

INFI∞ITY
PUBLISHING.COM

519 West Lancaster Avenue
Haverford, PA 19041-1413
Info@buybooksontheweb.com
www.buybooksontheweb.com
Toll-free (877) BUY BOOK
Local Phone (610) 520-2500
Fax (610) 519-0261

Printed in the United States of America

Printed on Recycled Paper

Published January 2003

In memory of a friend in the deepest sense
of the word – one who roamed with me
through many miles and many years,

Martha Haugh

And

Nan

For giving me the idea for the book.

Chapter 1

PEASE RIVER ON MULE CREEK NEAR MARGUERITE, TEXAS.
MAY 10,1836

Peta Nocona, the son of Iron Shirt, a Comanche War Chief, was a young warrior who on two raids had shown bravery and had counted coup. He and three warriors were sent out as scouts by Iron Shirt. They replaced the warriors who guarded the camp all night. He knew this was a tiresome job; his raven eyes were always watching the horizon, searching for something out of place. He lay hidden on top of the hill looking into the morning sun. He could now and then pick out the image of three riders. When he was sure, he signaled the scout on his right. The other three moved slowly under cover of the hill without raising any dust. Peta watched and waited until he recognized the riders.

"Little Foot, ride to Iron Shirt. Tell him three riders are headed this away. We will wait and ride in with them." He never took his eyes off the riders. The Kiowa slowed their pace. Each rider was leading a tired looking horse covered with dust and sweat. This made him believe they had ridden a long distance in a short time.

"It is time we mount and ride to meet them," Peta commanded as he ran and jumped on his horse. He and the other two braves rode over the hill straight toward the Kiowa. He stopped a short distance before reaching the three strangers, held his hand in the air to show a sign of peace and greeting.

"They call me Kicking Bird," the Kiowa in front said. The other two braves sat quietly behind him. "We are messengers from Chief Satank of the Kiowa with a message for Chief Iron Shirt's band and all the other Comanche bands. We have been riding four days to reach you."

"Come. We will take you into camp so you can talk to Iron Shirt," Peta said, as he moved along side of Kicking Bird. They rode together and the other warriors followed. The Comanche camp was large. It stretched a long way with scattered trees of cottonwood and live oaks with thickets of plum bushes, grapevines, and persimmons.

Peta led the Kiowa through the camp. In front of the largest tepee constructed of tanned buffalo hides stood Iron Shirt. Beside him stood

1

Little Foot. Peta and Kicking Bird dismounted. As they walked toward the tepee where a large group had gathered, the crowd opened and let them pass through.

Peta, now followed by Kicking Bird, stood in front of Iron Shirt. Kicking Bird raised his dusty hand and said, "I bring you greetings from Chief Satank of the Kiowa. Chief Satank wishes that I tell you he will call a war council seven suns from today. Chief Satank will hold the council at the junction of Elm Fork and West Fork of the Trinity River. Satank has invited all the Comanche and Caddo to join the Kiowa in a raid on Fort Parker. It is a council against the Whites from the south and east who are claiming our lands, stealing our horses, raiding our camps, and killing our women and children. I am also instructed to ask if you will send the message on to the other Comanche bands."

"I will send the message on to the other Comanche bands. Peta, take these warriors and feed them so they may rest."

Peta led Kicking Bird and the warriors toward his tepee when Kicking Bird slowed the pace. Smiling, he asked, "Are you married?"

"No, but I have my own tepee and a beautiful Mexican captive who is a good cook. My father gave me horses to trade for a wife, but I never found one I like. Are you married?"

"Yes, two summers ago."

"Do you have children?"

"No, but I have hope that we will soon because a man needs sons to carry on."

Peta stopped at the next tepee and said with a grin, "This is Sensa; she will feed and take care of you."

He left with the Kiowa horses so they could rest and graze. The horses were as tired as the men who rode them. He returned to his tepee after leaving the horses with the horse herder. He found that the Kiowa had their fill of food and water. Peta said smiling, "Kicking Bird, you will sleep in my tepee since it's small. I will find another place for your friends." He led the two Kiowa across camp to a tepee. In front sat an older woman sewing hides together. "Gray Foot, your son, Iron Shirt, wishes these braves to rest as they have traveled far."

Gray Foot's face turned from a withered look into a look of joy and happiness. Peta knew he hadn't told Gray Foot the truth, but by telling her Iron Shirt said it made his grandmother happy.

"Tell Iron Shirt that I will treat them well."

He heard the camp crier going through the camp calling for a council meeting of all the chiefs, and hurried toward the Live Oak tree known as the council tree. Since Iron Shirt had called the council, he would be the Chief in charge. The chiefs were all seated in a circle. Seated on Iron Shirt's right was Asa, a Peace Chief, and other elders. In the rest of the circle were all the chiefs seated in the order of their records of leadership, skill, and bravery. The people of the camp had formed an outer circle. Peta stood with the other braves behind the chiefs.

***

Iron Shirt rose, standing silent for a moment. Even the wind stood still. He looked at each of the lesser chiefs and said, "By now you all know about the message that we have received from Chief Satank. He has asked our help to raid the white settlement, the main one being Fort Parker. It is from this Fort Parker that the Whites are trading horses and making payment in bad money. They are also raiding both the Kiowa and the Caddo. This raid will take place in the Kiowa lands. If the Whites aren't stopped, they will just keep pushing westward until they reach our hunting grounds. Look, also, at what is happening in the south around San Antonio. The Whites are fighting the Mexicans, running them off their lands. The Whites are a people who we cannot trust. I feel forced to lead a war party to join with Chief Satank. Anyone who wishes to join me can do so." Iron Shirt stood silent for a while, started to speak again, but stopped and seated himself. Asa, a Peace Chief, was the next to speak. "If we join Satank, then the Whites can start raiding Comancheria. The tribes together can stop the westward movement of the Whites, to protect the Comanche hunting grounds. As Peace Chief, I ask the council to select the chiefs that are to stay behind. They will be able to protect the camp and continue with the buffalo hunt. The hunt is important this time of the year. The cows are shedding their winter hair that makes hides easier to tan and those hides make the best tepee covers. The ones who stay behind aren't cowards for not joining the War Party."

Iron Shirt listened to the chiefs as they spoke. Some of the chiefs spoke of the past, avoiding the present issue.

* * *

It was time for High Wolf to speak. Chief High Wolf, like Iron Shirt, had led many successful raids against the Comanche enemies. High Wolf stood but remained silent, and no one moved or spoke for over half an hour. He looked at each chief around the circle, his eyes fierce, and said, "Who is better to lead us than Iron Shirt? How many times in the past has Iron Shirt led us always in the lead of an attack ahead of the rest of us. His strong medicine always scares our enemies with his iron shirt. He draws their fire towards himself and away from us. Which of you can talk of such bravery?"

* * *

Iron Shirt was pleased when the council chose him to lead the War Party and selected the chiefs that were to stay. He stood. "All the chiefs who wish to join me on this raid, meet at my tepee." The camp crier rode through the camp crying the council decision. Iron Shirt returned to his tepee. His four wives sat cooking a buffalo hump over the open fire. His wives were cutting the meat into large chunks placing it on sticks four feet long. Each woman held the meat stick in a forked limb stuck in the ground. They easily rotated the meat stick over the fire of red hot coals. After the women warmed the meat, they stuck the sticks into the ground. The sweet aroma of the cooked meat filled the air.

Iron Shirt knew some chiefs wouldn't join him, so he was surprised at the number that showed up at his tepee. The group was too large to fit inside the tepee. He led the group past the fire to where the cooked meat rested, stopped at the first stick, and cut off a morsel of the meat. He then offered it to the Great Spirit by holding it first towards the sky and then burying the morsel in the ground. The chiefs gathered around the sticks, cutting off and eating the freshly cooked meat.

When the chiefs had eaten their fill, they followed him under the shade of a cottonwood tree whose leaves danced in the light breeze. He must explain what he expected of the chiefs. He sat facing the east, the chiefs completing the circle next to him.

"Tonight, I will send out scouts. After the war dance, we will meet in the cottonwood grove on the Pease. The main body will leave after midnight. This will give us five days to reach the Kiowa's Camp. We should arrive one day before the council meets. Each of your warriors should have two horses, his arms, and food packed well for so it's easy to carry. This is emergency ration only for our return trip. The scouts will provide us with fresh meat on our trip to the Kiowa's Camp. As soon as the raid is over, we want to put as much distance between the fort and ourselves."

Iron Shirt filled his sacred pipe with tobacco mixed with crushed sumac leaves and lifted it towards the sky to the Great Spirit. Sikway, his first wife and mother of Peta, stood behind him, and handed him a glowing reddish ember from the fire. He lit his pipe and passed it to his right. A chief not wanting to go on the raid would pass the pipe on without smoking it. Every chief smoked the pipe before passing it on.

4

He was well pleased. This gave him more encouragement that his medicine was strong and that his guardian spirit, the coyote, was with him. He regarded the coyote as his brother. Many times, in a vision before a battle, the coyote would speak of events to occur later in battle.

As the chiefs were leaving, he called to Chief High Wolf to stay. "It will please me much if you will lead your warriors as scouts. If anything happens to me you will take over as their leader."

"That is a great honor. I only hope that I can live up to your expectations."

Iron Shirt found a stick and started drawing in the loose dirt. "This is the Pease River. We will follow it down to Red River, following the Red until it bends back almost to itself. There we will turn south to the Trinity River."

"I know the place you mean. I was there last year."

"Since you have honored me by leading the scouts, I will honor your group by letting them dance first after the parade because you have to leave earlier. I am sending Peta, Kicking Bird, and the Kiowa with you. Kicking Bird can help you choose the route and Peta needs the experience. I will appreciate it if you work Peta hard."

"I will treat him as if he were my son," High Wolf said, turning to leave Iron Shirt.

"Will you find Peta and the Kiowa and tell them that they are to ride with you?"

"I will tell them."

Iron Shirt entered his tepee for it was time to prepare himself for the dance. Sikway was already under the bed pulling out his war bag, his shield, his lances, and his iron shirt. She carried his painted shield and lances outside the tepee. There she made a tripod of the lances, hanging the shield so it would absorb the all powerful medicine of the sun. Inside the tepee she opened his war bag on the bed. Sikway painted a black line across his forehead, then two black lines under his eyes and a red line under his mouth. She brushed his hair, greasing it and parting it down the middle of his forehead. She painted a yellow stripe down his part and braided a scalp lock at the top of his head and braided the sides. She then wrapped the braids with soft fur and tied red ribbons around it. She placed three feathers in the scalp lock, a yellow, a black, and an eagle feather. She gave him his iron shirt that had been handed down for generations. The shirt had been a part of gear worn by the Spanish Conquistadors. The old iron shirt had overlapping pieces of steel made like shingles on a roof. She helped Iron Shirt put the shirt on; he was dressed for the dance. Sikway picked up his empty war bag, placed it under their bed, and pulled out a drum which she handed to Iron Shirt and left the tepee. Iron Shirt began to drum and sing war songs.

* * *

Peta could hear drums playing all over the camp. He knew that the chiefs joining Iron Shirt were drumming and singing their war songs. The warriors were preparing for the raid. When they finished, they went to their leader's tepee and joined in the singing of the war songs. Peta had painted his face and his body to his waist. In his hair he braided a scalp lock with one black feather stuck in it. He joined the group of warriors at High Wolf's tepee.

Before sundown the drumming and singing stopped. The War Chiefs and warriors mounted and rode out of camp. They rode to the west end of the camp where he found High Wolf assembling his warriors, who lined up according to their standing in the band.

Iron Shirt led off this parade that signified the party was leaving that night. The warriors paraded in single file four times through the camp. Peta rode double, with a young warrior mounted behind, to show that he had carried a wounded or dismounted comrade out of battle to safety. The parade gave recognition to warriors for achievement in battle. As darkness fell upon the camp the parade ended.

He watched spectators make their way around a big fire in the center of the camp. They formed a circle around the fire leaving an opening for the dancers to enter. Only braves that were going on the raid could dance, aided by a woman partner. Before the dancers entered the circle, the drums stopped as Iron Shirt entered.

"All who are joining me on this raid with the Kiowa and Caddo on Fort Parker must display courage on raid so that your family may be proud of you and not consider you a coward. Since High Wolf's group is the scouting party, they will dance first," Iron Shirt said as his commanding voice broke the silence of the cool evening air.

Peta and Sensa, his Mexican captive, and his partner, entered the dance. After a few minutes had passed, Iron Shirt's group blended in with the dancers. He noticed that Iron Shirt and High Wolf silently left the dance. Knowing they were preparing to leave on the raid, he said something to Sensa who only grinned and nodded her head 'yes'. They left the dance. Sensa turned in the opposite direction of their tepee. He walked straight to his tepee where he picked up his gear for the trip, left his tepee, and took the path that led to his horses. As he walked past a thicket an arm shot out and grabbed him. The arm belonged to Sensa and before anyone could see, they were hiding in a thicket of plum bushes.

There they remained quiet because they could hear movement on all sides. A twig very quietly snapped.

Everyone in the camp understood what was going on in the brush, but the couples couldn't be seen together. He looked at the sky and realized it was time to leave. "I must go now," he said, standing. Sensa stood holding his hands.

"Take care of yourself, so you can return to me."

"Don't worry. I will be back before you know it." Peta moved quietly out of the brush.

He arrived at the cottonwood grove. Most of High Wolf's scouts were there. Standing by the fire was Kicking Bird. He walked over beside him, "Did you get rested up? You were gone when I picked up my gear."

"Yes, I wish to thank you for everything, especially for the one you sent me."

"What do you mean? I sent no one."

"Well, someone slipped into my bed when the dance started. When we arrive at my camp, I will pay you back ."

"That will not be necessary because I didn't send anyone." He wondered who it could have been. Maybe it was one of his mystery women who visited him at night because he knew it couldn't have been Sensa. She was at the parade and he was with her when the dance started.

High Wolf called his scouts together for it was time to leave. The raiding party had to leave before daylight, because for a war party to leave during daylight was bad medicine. At midnight High Wolf's scouts were checking the route ahead. He and Kicking Bird rode right beside High Wolf. High Wolf let Kicking Bird pick their way and was always sending him to the right or left.

Chapter 2

FORT PARKER ON THE NAVASOTA RIVER NEAR GROESBECK, TEXAS.

MAY 14, 1836.

Cynthia Ann Parker, ten years old with golden blond hair, walked beside Silas. "Are you going to the fields today, Daddy?"

"No, your Uncle Benjamin and I are working on tools that need fixing and we have other work to finish on the fort."

"Why did we run from the Mexican Calvary? Mamma told me that you built the fort to protect us from people who didn't like us."

"We ran because the Mexican Cavalry had artillery with them. They could blow big holes in the fort walls. We built the fort to protect us from the Indians."

"I was scared when we ran from the Mexicans, but I was really scared when we reached the Trinity and it was flooded."

"I know, dear! We were all scared. If Santa Anna hadn't thought that he had General Houston cornered on the San Jacinto River, we would have been trapped."

"What will we do if the Indians attack us?"

"We will shut the gate to keep them out and man the blockhouses. Eight men with the women loading the rifles can hold off hundreds of Indians. We built it like most eastern forts, having a bullet-proof gate and twenty foot walls with block houses on the opposite corners of the rectangle. It was built so each of the four blockhouses overhang the wall. The men firing from the blockhouses can protect all four walls."

She and Silas reached the first cabin just inside the gate. On a bench in front of his cabin sat Elder John, her grandfather, who usually spends his mornings reading the Bible. Stopping, she sat beside him in the warm sun.

"What are you reading this morning, Grandfather?"

"St. Mark 16: 15 'And he said unto them, Go ye all the world and preach the gospel to every creature'."

"That's the same one you were reading yesterday morning."

"It's a passage that we sure don't want to forget."

She sat quietly watching the men leave for the fields while Elder John continued reading to her from his Bible. She still was thinking about an Indian attack... how her father had been in charge of the Rangers, but he resigned. Now, her Uncle James was in charge of the fort's security. She overheard her mother and father talking about it one night in bed but didn't completely understand what they were talking about Her Uncle Daniel Parker was a delegate to the General Convention held at Washington-on-the-Brazos. The convention appointed Stephen Austin Commander-in-Chief. Daniel offered a resolution creating a company of Texas Rangers. The convention set up two companies of volunteer Rangers with twenty-five volunteers to a company. They appointed her father as Superintendent of the Rangers. Silas was to guard the frontiers between the Brazos and Trinity Rivers. He soon found out that the volunteers wouldn't follow orders. The Rangers would attack any Indian on sight. It was causing more trouble on the frontier than they were solving. The Indians attacked the Rangers while on their regular patrol. Five of the Rangers received wounds and one was killed. Silas asked for a surgeon to accompany his Rangers, but the general council turned him down. So, Silas resigned. Daniel Parker, his brother, sent a message that some Whites on Grimes Prairie were stealing horses from the Caddo near Waco. Daniel believed that they were going on the war path. Silas knew he couldn't control his men. His brother, James, accepted the position because he believed he could.

James' pregnant daughter, Rachel Plummer, came trudging along dragging James Platt, who was two years old, his bare feet toddling in the dust. "Cynthia Ann, your mother said for you to get home and see if you can find John. She has her hands full with Silas M. Jr. and Orlena. She is baking bread and can't leave," Rachel said, walking right on past them and inside Elder John's cabin. She walked down the center of the fort looking for John. The cabins were built in two rows against the fort's north and south walls. Elizabeth Duty Kellogg and Sally Frost were making soap. Elizabeth was stirring the kettle of lye and fat. Sally was placing more wood on the fire. Her children were with her; one was in the cradle and the other playing on the ground. Cynthia Ann liked the smell of wood smoke and walked towards them.

"Have you seen John this morning?" Cynthia Ann asked.

"I saw him earlier. He was down by the corral," Sally said, as she stuck a feather into the kettle stirring it around.

"Why did you put the feather in there?"

"See how the bristles are damaged? The lye is too strong. We need to add more fat or it will eat our hands up when we use it".

She saw her mother looking in her direction and moved quickly on looking for John. Martha Duty Parker and her daughter, Sarah Parker Nixon, were washing clothes. They had three large black iron pots; two were filled with cold water. The third sat over a fire filled with boiling water containing lye soap. Martha was rinsing the clothes in the cold water to soak and remove the dirt. She then placed them on a slatted table, beating them dry with a paddle. Sarah was stirring the clothes in hot boiling lye water with a paddle. After they boiled for a while, Sarah put them in the clear water pot. Martha rinsed the clothes, then beat them dry with the paddle before hanging them up to finish drying.

She found John beside George and Rebecca Dickens' cabin playing with the Dickens' two boys. George had killed a deer and was now skinning it. Old Man Lumm was helping him cut it up.

"Well, Cynthia Ann, we are going to have fresh meat tonight," George said. "Soon as we get it cut up Lumm and I will deliver it. Lumm isn't sure if the Faulkenberries, Bates, and Anglins are coming into the fort tonight."

"John, you run home and tell mother where you have been," Cynthia Ann said, watching the men cut up the deer.

"I personally think they will stay at their cabins tonight because they are behind in planting. The time we spent running from the Mexican Cavalry was costly," Lumm said, finishing cutting up his half.

"Why do the Anglins, Bates, Faulkenberries and you have cabins outside the fort?" she asked.

"It was in July 1834 that your father, Silas, and your Uncle James joined Elish Anglins in staking out their claims. We staked our claims on east of the fort close to your Uncle James' claim," Lumm answered.

"I remember that. We were living at Fort Houston then in our wagon," she replied.

"That's right. The fort was built on your father's claim and the land your family farms was on your Uncle James' claim. Anglin's cabin and claim was a mile farther east. Later, the Bates, Faulkenberries and I came, so we built cabins closer to our farms, also. We all keep many of our possessions here in the fort in the blockhouses. Sometimes when we get to feeling there may be danger from the Indians, we all sleep in the fort those nights. I feel safe inside the fort because it's well built and at night the gates are always closed. That's why we spend our nights inside," Lumm remarked, while he spread the deer hide on the table scraping the green hide free of flesh. Cynthia Ann decided that she had better hurry home because the water barrel needed filling.

She saw her mother, Lucy, cut the end off of a loaf of fresh baked bread and drop it on the ground for Dog. She remembered when her mother found the dog and had never named him. Her mother just called him "Dog" because when she found him she wasn't sure he was going to live. Lucy found him in the grass starved at a campsite that many wagon trains had used. She fed him some scraps of left over meat. Dog was so weak that he didn't eat much. Lucy wrapped him up in her old coat and put him in the front of the wagon. Every time they stopped to rest the oxen, she would feed him a little more with a drink of water. Lucy kept the children away from him while he recovered. Dog never did make friends with her and John. John treated him terribly and squeezed him too hard as he carried him around. Dog was their mother's dog and never left her side.

Lucy cut a slice of the fresh baked bread for John and her. Her mother only smiled at her when she picked up the bread and the wooden water bucket and hurried away towards the spring. It was a rare occasion that Lucy needed to tell her to get her work done. She loved to visit with the others in the fort, but always worked hard until she finished her chores.

Cynthia Ann didn't know whether to eat the bread or just smell it. Inside the back door of the Fort, she paused to watch Roberta Frost churn the butter. Roberta's movement of the dasher up and down in an exact rhythm made her want to dance. The Frost's two girls were planting in their make-believe garden. She went out the back gate of the Fort swinging the bucket as she walked to the spring. As she bent over dipping the bucket into the water, she saw a blurred image of a man standing behind her. She was so scared she couldn't move. He had no clothes on and two feathers were sticking out his head. She turned around quickly dropping the bucket, but there was no one there. Shaking, she grabbed the bucket and hurried back into the fort.

She returned with the water and saw that John was doing his job. John's job was to watch Silas Jr. and rock Orlena's cradle whenever she cried. Silas Jr. was sitting on the ground digging dirt with a stick. John played with a pop gun that Elder John made for him. He was always shooting Indians. John had never seen an Indian, but he had heard stories about them from Elder John.

11

Chapter 3

Iron Shirt's warriors arrived on Elm Fork before sundown and made camp with the other Comanche bands. His Noconis band camped with the other Comanche bands: Penatekas, Kotsatekas, Quahadas, and Yamparikas. The Comanche Chiefs of all bands met in council and agreed that Iron Shirt should speak for the Comanche. One Chief from each band would serve as a delegate and advisor.

"We should all go now and honor Chief Satank with our presence," Iron Shirt said. "We need to tell him that together we have more than two hundred warriors ready for the attack."

"Iron Shirt, I see that you brought extra horses with you like the rest of us. Do you have plans for after the raid, where we should meet and pick up our horses and gear?" Chief Howes of the Yamparikas band blurted out.

"We will ask Satank where he has planned to meet after the raid to split the boody."

"If the Caddo and Kiowa have as many warriors as we have, I only hope there's enough booty to go around," remarked Shaking Hand of the Kotsatekas.

"I'm sure he will not want to return here because, if they follow us, our trail would lead them straight to his camp," Chief Bull Hump of Penatekas replied.

"Let's go now and see Chief Satank. Maybe he will provide us with more answers. Tonight could be the last rest we will get for awhile," Chief Wild Horse of the Quahadas exclaimed.

The Chiefs started for the Kiowa's Camp and were overtaken by Kicking Bird and Peta. "I was on my way to lead you to Chief Satank. I'm taking Peta to my tepee, so he can enjoy the comfort of home tonight," Kicking Bird said.

"Well, before you and Peta get too comfortable, take us to you Chief Satank."

* * *

Kicking Bird and Peta led the way through the camp. The people looked at them and then returned to whatever they were doing. When they arrived at Chief Satank's tepee, Kicking Bird announced that Chief Iron Shirt was there with the other Comanche Chiefs. Satank rushed to the tepee opening, greeted Iron Shirt as a brother, and then asked the Chiefs to enter his tepee.

Kicking Bird led Peta to the other side of camp to his tepee. Kicking Bird motioned Peta to follow him inside. "This is my wife, Adeca, and her sister, Red Dress. We call her Red Dress because you can see all the red ribbons tied in her hair and on her deerskin dress." Kicking Bird and Peta sat facing the door behind the small bed of coals in the center of the tepee. The sisters busied themselves cooking meat on sticks over the fire. The small fire made dancing forms on the sides of the tepee. Peta watched Red Dress who was facing him and their eyes met several times. They smiled at each other. Kicking Bird gave a small unseen nod to Adeca to signify that Peta and Red Dress liked each other.

After they ate, Kicking Bird showed Peta around the camp and stopped at his parents' tepee. Kicking Bird introduced Peta to his father, mother, and his grandfather, No-Name. Peta asked, after they are a distance away from the tepee, "Why is your grandfather called No-Name?"

"He was a great warrior when he was younger and named Kicking Bird, but like your people, it is a taboo to speak the name of a dead one. When I was old enough to join the Rabbit Society, he worked and trained me. Later I was eligible to join the Military Society. He gave me his name Kicking Bird and took the name No-Name."

"That shows great respect when he gave you his name."

"I only hope that I can live up to his expectations."

They slowly made their way back to Kicking Bird's tepee, and found the women were in bed. Kicking Bird showed Peta to the bed on the opposite side.

* * *

Peta realized then that Red Dress was in the bed in the back of the tepee. Peta removed his shirt, breechclout, moccasins, and leggings, then crawled between the buffalo robes. Falling asleep, he was awakened by a soft hand rubbing his body. The heat of the two bodies under the robe was more than he could stand. He started to throw the robe off when she raised and moved over him. The rush of fresh air and his excitement made him forget that he was sweating. When it was over she laid beside him and he held her tenderly in his arms. Peta woke before daylight, and he was alone in his bed. He looked around the room. Everyone was still asleep, but he knew it was Red Dress who visited his bed because of the ribbons in her hair.

He hurried, dressed, and left Kicking Bird's tepee for Iron Shirt's Camp where he was greeted by High Wolf.

"It's good you are here because we are ready to leave. Select the horse from the herd that you will ride tomorrow and your extra gear. We are to help the horse herders move to where we will meet them after the raid," High Wolf said.

He moved quickly, got his gear, and selected his horse when Kicking Bird rode up. "You left early this morning,"

"High Wolf. didn't think so."

"He is not going any place until we lead him to the place. Did you sleep well?"

"Yes, I did, but you didn't have to provide me with such pleasures. I wasn't expecting it."

"What happened to you last night was your doing, not mine. Red Dress lives with us now since her parents were killed."

"How were they killed?"

"We moved our camp to this location. It was necessary to build a new medicine lodge. It was the job of the Bear Women Society to cut cottonwood poles and branches. Their men will go with them and drag the poles back to camp while the women ride behind them. The girl's parents were returning when the men from Fort Parker attacked, killing them both."

The Kiowa sat a faster pace so they rode in silence. They were riding west with the sun on their backs. By mid-morning they arrived at a grassy valley with a stream running down the middle. The outer hills were high from which you could see miles in both directions. Here they left their extra gear and horses with both Comanche and Kiowa guarding them.

They returned to the Kiowa's Camp, and made their way to the council meeting. Chief Satank was speaking in the center of a large circle of chiefs with the delegates seated behind. Peta and Kicking Bird were well to the back standing with the other spectators.

"You all know Manual Flores who has traded with us for years. He wishes to speak to us as a Mexican agent for the Mexican Government. We do well to listen to what he has to say," Satank shouted for all to hear.

Peta moved closer to get a better look at the Mexican agent. Manual stood, took off his Mexican sombrero, placed it on the ground, so everyone could see his face clearly, and walked slowly to the center of the council circle. With fierce eyes, he announced angrily, "The Anglos swore allegiance as citizens of the Republic of Mexico. They have broken this promise with the attack on the Alamo at San Antonio. They have defeated Santa Anna's Army at San Jacinto. The Anglos will not stop until they have all of Texas. Stephen Austin went to Washington asking for help, supplies, and a loan to support the new Republic of Texas. The Anglos all help each other and you will find in a few years all the tribes of Texas will be fighting the Anglos. I am authorized by the Mexican Government to give you legal title to the land and supply you with guns and ammunition, if you promise to drive the Anglos out of Texas. I will talk to the individual chiefs of each band after the raid on Fort Parker."

The chiefs who were in doubt about the need of the raid on the fort now had changed their minds. Iron Shirt rose to speak. "I have a plan that will guarantee the success of the raid on the fort without losses. The Wacos tell me they have traded horses with a James Parker and he cheats them with bad money, and then they are punished for having the bad money."

"Why should we let you lead the raid, so the Comanche get all the booty?" Chief Sky Walker, a subchief of the Kiowa, announced angrily.

"We, the Comanche, will let you split all the booty except the captives. We need women captives because our women are only having one or two children. Most of them are girls. Our chiefs have no sons to carry on the family name," Iron Shirt remarked as he sat down.

The Kiowa Chiefs were talking softly among themselves. Finally, Chief Sky Walker questioned again. "Iron Shirt, how do we know you have a good plan?"

Iron Shirt rose slowly choosing his words carefully, and with a commanding voice said, "Your Chief Satank knows me and my word is good, but I pledge to you that your braves shall be the first inside the fort without a shot being fired, if you will follow my orders."

Before another chief could speak, Satank announced bluntly, "Iron Shirt has spoken straight and his medicine is strong and I believe him."

Chief Satank's comments quieted the Kiowa chiefs. They didn't push the leadership of the raid any farther. The chiefs all agreed that Iron Shirt should lead the raid. Chief Satank said, "The war party will leave for Fort Parker at midnight."

Chapter 4

FORT PARKER NEAR GROESBECK, TEXAS.

MAY 19, 1836

Iron Shirt moved the four hundred Comanche, Kiowa, and Caddo into the woods north of the fort. Iron Shirt sat on his horse and watched as the men from the fort left for the fields. He gave orders the night before to High Wolf, who was to lead the Comanche, and to Sky Walker, who would lead the Kiowa and the other Indian Chiefs. Sky Walker was to lead his braves into the fort, and High Wolf was to lead his braves around the back of the fort. This would happen only on Iron Shirt's command.

Iron Shirt raised his lance in the air and the Indians moved slowly towards the fort. They rode quietly until he raised his lance again; the group of Indians stopped. There were still Indians moving out of the wooded area to join the group. Iron Shirt tied a dirty white flag on his lance and he and Sky Walker rode towards the fort. The fort's large heavy gate was open. Iron Shirt saw most of the people going about their daily jobs. He stopped two hundred yards in front of the gate and sat quietly on his horse.

* * *

Elder John heard someone yell, "Indians! Indians!" Looking around he saw Sarah Nixon slip out the back door. He was hoping that Sarah was leaving to get her husband, Levin, and her father, James. Elder John shouted at Cynthia Ann, "Get home to your mother!"

Elder John hurried towards the gate where Benjamin and Silas stood, "I am going to find out what they want since they are carrying a flag of truce," Benjamin said quietly. "I have never seen a war bonnet that has so many colors. He is new to this area. I have traded horses and other goods with the Kiowa and I have been on friendly terms with them. But the Indian with a shirt that shines in the sun, looks like the Chief. And the way he sits proudly on his horse staring at the fort, scares me. I will be right back."

"No, shut the gate! There are five of us men and if they want a fight, we will sell our lives dearly," Silas yelled, pushing on the gate. The gate was too heavy to close because it took three men, and Silas and Elder John were alone at the front of the fort. Benjamin was already outside.

"They will kill him," Elder John snapped loudly as he watched. Benjamin stood talking to Iron Shirt who sat very straight holding his spear very rigid in the air for all to see. Benjamin and Sky Walker were using sign language. Benjamin suddenly dropped his arm in disgust and turned towards the fort.

"Thank God, the Indians didn't kill him," Elder John whispered softly.

"They say they're without food and want a cow. They also need directions to a spring," Benjamin stated, glaring back at the Chief with the shining shirt.

"We aren't giving them a cow," Elder John growled. "A cow wouldn't feed that many Indians; maybe ten cows would. You can't tell me those Indians don't know where the springs are."

"I believe they intend to fight," Benjamin replied. "I will go back and see if I can talk them out of it; but just in case, you get the fort ready for a fight."

"Shut the gate!" Silas roared. The sound fell on deaf ears because Benjamin had left the fort for the Indians.

Rachel Plummer ran out the door of Elder John's cabin dragging her son, James Platt, when Silas yelled at her, "You stay here and watch the Indians until I run home and get my other shot bag." Silas saw Samuel Frost and his son, Robert, running towards the main gate. He saw George Dickens running for the back gate followed by his family and the Frost family.

"Good Lord, Dickens, you aren't going to run, are you?" Silas yelled.

"No, I am only going to try to hide the women and children in the woods."

"Dickens, stand and fight like a man, and if we have to die, we will sell our lives as dearly as we can."

Rachel turned toward the gate and watched Benjamin walking toward the Indians. When Benjamin reached Iron Shirt raised his lance into the air. The raid on Fort Parker had began. The Indians surrounded Benjamin and killed him on the spot.

* * *

Sky Walker's braves dismounted along the east wall of the fort. Iron Shirt's signal was the sign for them to attack the front gate. The blood-chilling yell of the Indians struck fear and panic into the residents of the fort. The Indians were pouring into the front gate and met Rachel with James Platt. Rachel grabbed a hoe, swinging it at a warrior who was reaching for James Platt. The warrior caught the hoe, jerked it out of Rachel's hands, and hit her on the forehead. The other Indians drove lances into Elder John, Samuel, and Robert Frost. Silas, carrying his unloaded gun, ran to Rachel's aid. He used the gun as a club to fight off the braves around Rachel. Silas knocked many of the braves to the ground, but there were too many for him by himself. Silas saw Granny Parker running out of her cabin towards the back of the fort. She was over taken, stripped of her dress and pinned to the ground with lances. Silas, with a spear sticking out of his back, fell to the ground.

High Wolf led his braves around the back of the fort to cut off the people running out the back door from reaching the brushy woods. Big Tree of the Kiowa led his braves and some Caddo around the other side. The Caddo braves took Elizabeth Kellogg captive. The braves took her to the front of the fort where Rachel and James Platt were held.

The Indians inside the fort were having a good time. They were searching every cabin looking for booty in old trunks, medicine bottles, rifles, gunpowder, and bullets. Brightly colored clothes were fought over by the finders. Books were high on the Indians' list of needs. They used the paper in the books to make their shields. A shield was made out of a buffalo hide by heating and steaming until it was thick. It was then packed with an inch of paper between the two thick hides.

They carried the feather mattresses outside, cutting them up and looking for something hidden. The feathers flew in the air like snow. They gathered up all the iron tools that were useful in making weapons. Any item they didn't want they tore up just for the fun of it.

* * *

Lucy Parker was carrying Orlena and pulling along Silas Jr. and John. Cynthia Ann, holding John's other hand, was pulling him along. Peta saw them, and raced his pony at top speed jerking Cynthia Ann upon the pony. He never slowed down, turning the pony with his knees. He looked back and a warrior was swinging John onto his pony and was riding hard behind him. They rode to where the captives were held. Peta stayed with Cynthia Ann and the other captives.

19

* * *

Cynthia Ann saw her Aunt Rachel, James Platt, Aunt Elizabeth, and John were also captives. Rachel had dried blood all over her face, and it made her sick to look at her. She knew she had to be brave because John was puckering up. Each time James Platt let out a cry, the guard would hit him. Rachel tried to quiet him and then the guard hit her. She wondered what happened to her father, mother, her sister, and her brother.

* * *

Sarah Nixon, by luck, made it past the Indians to the fields without being seen. James, her father, Levin Nixon, her husband, and Luther Plummer, her brother-in-law, heard her screaming and ran toward her. Sarah told them the fort was surrounded by Indians. James Parker sent Plummer to tell the other men in their fields a half-mile away. James and Nixon, unarmed, headed for the fort. They were half-way to the fort when they ran into James' wife and children. Nixon agreed with James that James should take his family away to safety. He led his family towards the Navasota River.

* * *

Lucy, running as hard as she could carrying Orlena and dragging Silas Jr., was worn out. Silas' short legs just couldn't keep up without the help of John and Cynthia Ann. As she looked back she saw the Indians were gaining on her. When an Indian on horseback made a pass at picking up Silas Jr., Lucy's dog had enough. He turned, jumped into the air, and grabbed the horse by the nose, throwing the rider into a gully. The Indians, on foot from the fort, were catching her. She thought it was all over for her and the children.

Luckily for her Levin Nixon emerged from the brush unarmed. His appearance slowed down the Indians. He quickly placed himself between the Indians and Lucy. The Indians, realizing Nixon was unarmed, rushed him.

* * *

At the same time, David Faulkenberry ascended from a ravine with his rifle. He knew if he fired a shot, the Indian would kill him before he could reload. He worked Nixon, Lucy, and the children behind himself. With them behind he could sweep the rifle more freely back and forth.

But the Indians were making dashes toward them and were closing the distance between Nixon, Lucy, and himself. He knew time was running out.

High Wolf's braves on horses were ready to attack in a group effort. Their goal was to kill David and Nixon, and then capture Lucy with the children. When Silas Bates, Abram Anglin, and Evan Faulkenberry, armed with rifles, stepped out of the brush, the five men formed in a ring around Lucy and the children. The braves backed off and started to regroup for attack when Luther Plummer, Rachel's husband, appeared with fifteen men.

* * *

Iron Shirt, not liking the odds now with no shots fired, decided it was a good time to quit. Iron Shirt raised his lance, moving it in a slow circle, to signal the Indians it was time to withdraw. The Indians left Fort Parker area as quietly and as quickly as they had appeared. The captives were placed in front of their captor as they rode away. Cynthia Ann was scared. Here she was, riding away from her family, and a bad smelling Indian had one arm around her holding her on his horse.

* * *

James Parker, Cynthia Ann's uncle, led his wife, Martha, and the children across the Navasota River. After taking them downstream, he hid them in dense briers. He left them and crossed back over the river. He was now downstream farther south than his field, and headed back towards the fort, stopping at Abram Anglin's cabin. There, he picked up a butcher knife. He ran into Dickens with his wife, Rebecca, and their four children. In the group was Roberta Frost with her four children, the smallest one still nursing, and Roberta's daughter-in-law, Sally, and her two children. He led the group across the river to where his family was hiding.

James' group now included six adults and twelve children who ranged from babies to twelve years old. The group remained hidden in the briers and underbrush. He waited until sundown, then climbed a tree. He could see the fort, but saw no movement nor heard any voices. He climbed down and turned to the group, "I'm going back to the fort. We need supplies, and I'll also check to see if anyone is alive."

"Please, James, don't leave us," his wife, Martha, answered.

"Dickens can take care of you till I return."

21

"James, you know I am not capable of leading this group to Tinnin's Settlement. I have no knowledge of where it's located," Dickens stood kicking the sand with his foot.

"Dickens, before this is over, you may have to lead this group, so start preparing yourself," he commented walking away. He stopped and turned back to the group, "We do need supplies. It is ninety miles to the Tinnin's Settlement."

"I would rather face starvation than have you leave us," Roberta replied with the others agreeing.

"We have no food and most of you are barefoot. We will have to stay close to the river in the briers and underbrush. You women and children aren't dressed for the cold nights and briers. It will be a hard journey--specially hard on you women still nursing children."

"We'll make it!" Roberta and Martha said in harmony.

He gave in to them and decided to travel after dark and remain concealed in the daytime. It was dark when James picked up one of youngest children and placed him on his shoulders and then took another one by the hand. The others followed his example and the group started through the entangled briers. The briers were tearing the children's shirts, and it was all they had on. Scratching their arms, legs and feet, they could be tracked by the drops of blood on the ground.

His group traveled until three o'clock in the morning. The women and children, hungry and exhausted, huddled together for warmth from the cool night air. He leaning against a tree and dozed until dawn.

Chapter 5

FORT PARKER NEAR GROESBECK, TEXAS.

MAY 20, 1836

"Lucy! are you, Orlena and Silas Jr. the only survivors from the Fort?" Luther Plummer asked.

"Lord! I don't know; everything happened so fast. They captured Cynthia Ann and John before Levin saved us."

"I'm going to see if I can find Rachel and James Platt," Luther said as he walked away. The men from the fields joined Lucy, everyone sat quietly, only talking in a whisper.

* * *

"It will be dark soon. What about you and me trying to get back to the fort?" Abram Anglin asked, looking straight at Evan Faulkenberry.

"That's fine with me, 'cause I hear it's bad medicine for Indians to attack after dark."

Together, they moved slowly and quietly out of the creek into the woods until they come to Abram's cabin just outside the fort. Abram went inside while Evan watched and listened.

"Well, at least they never got this far south," Abram said, standing in the doorway. The night was dark because the sky was cloudy, but now and then streaks of light filtered through. They started for the fort.

As Abram and Evan came nearer the fort, they saw a figure of a ghost crawling along the ground. It was dressed in white and had long white hair. Abram ran behind a tree and Evan ducked behind another. Looking around the trees it looked like the ghost was beckoning them to come forward.

"What is it?" Evan asked with fear in his voice. He was ready to run. Whatever it was he wanted no part of the ghostly creature.

"You stay here and cover me with your gun and I will circle behind it." As Abram moved through the trees, he was more scared at that moment than when the Indians were charging at him and the others. He crept up behind the still white figure. As he started to move closer, a cloud passed, and a ray of light shone on the ghost.

"It's a body!" he yelled as he ran forward to where the body lay. "My God, it's Granny Parker, but she is still alive!"

"What are we going to do? She's hurt bad. Both of her sides are drenched with blood".

"I don't see any fresh blood so the wounds must have sealed over. You stay here. I'll go back to my cabin and bring back some blankets."

Abram returned with two blankets. They placed Granny on one of the blankets and carried her to a good hiding place. Evan covered her up with the other blanket.

"She's lost a lot of blood. Do you think she'll be all right?"

"We have to leave her here until we return from the fort. Maybe we can find someone there still alive."

"Abram," Granny said in a low whisper, "When you get to the fort, beside my cabin there is a small hickory bush. You will find buried on the south side $106.50 in silver."

"I'll get it for you, Granny. Right now you rest and lie quiet until we get back. Evan, come on and let's see what other surprises are in store for us."

As Abram and Evan worked their way closer to the fort, they heard cattle bawling, dogs barking, horses neighing, and hogs squealing. They couldn't find anyone else alive. Afraid the Indians were still close, they hurried back to Granny and gave her the silver bag.

Taking the top cover, they placed it on the ground and picked up the cover that Granny was lying on and placed it on top. The two covers gave Granny good support. They carried her back to the others at the creek. There, Lucy, Cynthia Ann's mother, and Sarah Nixon, James' daughter, bandaged her wound and made her as comfortable as possible.

At daylight Abram Anglin, Silas Bates, and Evan Faulkenberry, all well-armed, went back to the fort. They caught six horses, but could only find three saddles and four bridles. They loaded three of the horses with corn meal, bacon, and honey. They quickly left the fort because they were still afraid the Indians would return.

Abram stopped at his cabin and picked up a heavy piece of canvas, rope, and an axe. Arriving back at the creek, the men all set to work making a travois to haul Granny. They cut two long straight hickory poles and tied them to the saddle horn on each side of the horse, then cut short poles of different lengths to make the cross pieces. The cross pieces were placed in the notches of the long poles and held in place by ropes. The heavy canvas was placed on top. Granny, wrapped in two blankets, was placed on the travois. The party started for Fort Houston. Lucy, Orlena, and Silas Jr. rode one horse while Sarah rode another, and Granny rode on the travois. The other three horses were loaded with the supplies.

* * *

James woke his group and led them away from the river to avoid the briers. He soon came upon Indian pony tracks. Scared that the Indians were still looking for the group, he turned back to the river. When the group came to sand, a place where they would leave tracks, he made them walk backwards. This was to fool the Indians into believing the group was headed for the fort. As they moved south the briers grew worse, but he thought the pain of the briers was a small price to pay for their lives.

His guilty feeling about the fort being attacked weighed heavily on his mind. If he hadn't discharged the Frontier Rangers and had stayed at the fort, maybe the events would have turned out differently. The fort could have held if they had only shut the gates. Why didn't Silas and Benjamin shut the gates? The men in the field would have heard the shooting and could have put the Indians in a cross fire.

At sundown, he stopped the group; they were all suffering from the lack of food. The women still nursing children were exhausted from hunger and fatigue. Their feet were sore, arms and legs cut. It was almost impossible for them to take another step. The group found a grassy spot and laid down.

`He walked over to the bank of the Navasota River looking down into the river bottoms. He saw a skunk moving in his direction, and waited until the skunk was directly below him. He missed landing on the skunk but as he grabbed for it, the skunk jumped into the water. He caught it and held it under water until it drowned. With Anglin's knife he butchered the skunk, built a small fire and cooked it. He equally divided the skunk among the group, which, unfortunately, was only a small amount of food for each.

He led his group for two more days. All the women and children were hungry and exhausted. The women still nursing babies could hardly move. He stopped the group early in the evening to go hunting. Again he killed a skunk and also found two small turtles.

25

The next morning the group's spirit was better as they had eaten and had a good night's sleep. He took off his shirt and tore it into strips. He wrapped the children's sore and bleeding feet with the strips. Dickens saw what James was doing, took off his shirt, and also helped wrapped the children's feet.

He led the group all day, finally stopping early in the evening. The group was totally exhausted from hunger and fatigue. Their feet were so sore it made it almost impossible for them to travel. The children were half naked-their clothes torn to shreds.

James looked the group over and decided they had only one chance of finishing the trip. He called to Dickens and led him away from the group. After they were out of hearing range James said, "Dickens, the group has had it. We are still ten miles from the Tinnin's Settlement. There is no way all of them in their condition can make it."

"But, James, what are we going to do?"

"If you will stay with them-just let them move at their own pace, I will leave in the morning for the Settlement."

"How will I know the way and not get them lost?"

"Stay close to the river. The Settlement is located on the Navasota straight south of here. I should be back with help sometime tomorrow."

He and Dickens went back to where the group was resting.

"I talked it over with Dickens and he will stay here and lead you to the Settlement. I will leave in the morning to get help, as it's not far. I should be back late tomorrow with help."

The children were asleep-the women didn't even raise their heads. All they wanted was sleep because in their sleep they could forget how tired and hungry they were. James grinned to himself for nobody argued with him this time.

He was up before sunrise and started his journey to the Settlement. He hadn't eaten anything for six days as he had given his share to the children. He was tired but stopped only for a drink of water. The thought of the tired hungry children drove him on. Many times he started to stagger, like a drunk, but his staggering was from lack of food.

It was early evening when he arrived at the Settlement. The first house he came to was Captain Carter's. He explained his predicament to Captain Carter. While he ate his first meal in six days, Captain Carter rounded up horses. The Captain returned with five horses and they immediately started back to find Dickens and the group.

It was almost dark when they found the group still plodding along. The only hope on their minds was every step moved them closer to food, and they all knew, if it was possible, he would be back. He was able to load the women and children on the horses for the return trip to the Settlement. It was midnight when the ragged, hungry group arrived at the Carters. Mrs. Carter and the ladies of the Settlement gathered up old clothes for the women and children to wear and prepared food for the starving group.

Chapter 6

EAGLE MOUNTAIN IN TARRANT COUNTY.

MAY 20, 1836

Cynthia Ann didn't know where they were as Sky Walker led the raiding party into the valley. She saw it was a camp for the extra horses and gear. The guards had a fire built and the cooks were roasting a deer on spits, turning the spits to cook the deer evenly.

She watched the riders jerk their captives off their horses. The captives were tied with a hair braided thong around their wrists and their hands behind their back. The Indians pushed them face down, all but her. She was lowered to the ground gently by Peta. He tied her ankles together and pulled her hands and feet together. A new guard came to replace Peta.

She could hear the others talking, then crying out with the pain. "Cynthia Ann, are you here?" Aunt Elizabeth asked. "Yes! I am here." As she said it, a guard hit her on the legs with a bow. She then realized if she was quiet, no one would hit her. She felt sorry for James Platt. James Platt kept calling for his mother, Rachel, and when she answered, they were both hit. Being only eighteen months old, he had never been treated that way before, nor had she and John ever been punished or treated like this. John hadn't made a sound. She couldn't see him and wondered if he was all right.

James Platt was still calling for his mother and she was answering him. The guards were hitting them both when Iron Shirt walked up. "Stop hitting the captives," he announced angrily to the braves, then turned and walked away.

Cynthia Ann didn't understand a word Iron Shirt said but felt better by listening to the sound of his firm voice. The captives all quieted down.

She watched as the Victory Dance was started by the combined tribes. The warriors danced around the fire screaming and stomping their feet in rhythm with the drums. Each warrior danced holding his most prized possession. They carried scalps, books, and guns. The ones who had taken captives, carried a personal item of that person. She saw that Peta was carrying her shoe that he took off when he tied her up.

* * *

Iron Shirt called all the chiefs together. He sat and listened while they told of the brave deeds that their followers accomplished. The chiefs agreed on which group surpassed the rest, and those chiefs were given first pick of the booty, but not of the captives. The warriors were given the captives that they had captured. When the chiefs were all in agreement, they moved to the other side of the fire where the booty was.

The chiefs selected the booty in the order chosen earlier, taking what they wanted but not too much. When all the chiefs had finished their selection, Iron Shirt made his selection. Again the chiefs made their selection in the same order until all the booty was gone.

He knew his medicine was strong because they had taken the fort without firing a shot. If he was to take too much, it could cause his medicine to fail. This also showed the other chiefs by giving freely, his medicine was strong. He could get more booty in other raids.

* * *

Cynthia Ann watched the Indians dance and celebrate until daylight. Peta came with a horse, untied Cynthia Ann, and placed her on the horse. He tied her wrists with a braided hair thong which he braided into the horse's mane. Peta tied her ankles together under the horse's stomach and then braided the lead rope from Cynthia Ann's horse into his horse's tail. She knew wherever Peta went, she was sure to follow.

Cynthia Ann saw how the other warriors prepared their captives for the trip. John and James Platt were both tied on their horses just like she was. Rachel and Elizabeth were stripped of all their clothing and tied on their horse.

For the next five days she and the other captives were led north through prairies scattered with woods. Every night the Indians stopped to build a fire and continued dancing and singing around it. She noticed that Peta gave her a larger portion of food and water than the others rceived. She watched women captives being abused, but the children received better care.

On the sixth morning she watched the tribes split into two groups. The Comanche, along with herself, John, James Platt, and Rachel headed northwest. The Kiowa and the Caddo headed east with Elizabeth. Both of the women were badly sunburned. She watched the owner of Rachel and Elizabeth smear their bodies with mud to keep their fiery red bodies from blistering.

She saw Rachel was riding closer to James Platt. When he saw his mother he cried, "Mama, Mama, Mama!" The Indians stopped, untied Rachel, and dragged her to the ground. They carried James Platt to her. She quickly embraced him in her arms as if she was nursing him. Rachel had weaned James Platt when she found out she was pregnant. James Platt wouldn't nurse in spite her efforts to make him do so. The Indians realized he was weaned and jerked him from her.

Cynthia Ann watched the Comanche bands split again taking

with them their captives. The Yamparikas crossed the Red River and headed northwest towards Colorado with Rachel. The Kotsatekas, with James Platt, Rachel's son, also crossed the Red River and turned west into the Panhandle of Texas. The Noconis, with her, followed the Red River. The Penatekas and Quahadas, with John, rode with the Noconis for one more day before turning south.

She didn't realize that they were camping a mile away from the Noconis camp. Little Foot rode away as Peta untied her. She no longer felt afraid of Peta because his eyes betrayed his harsh voice. She was free to walk around the camp and no one paid any attention to her or bothered her.

She saw all warriors were rubbing their horses down with grass. Cynthia Ann, after eating, found a spot of soft grass and laid down. She expected Peta would come to tie her up for the night, but when she awoke the next morning she found that she hadn't been tied up. The camp was full of excitement. All the Indians were putting on their war paint and war dress. Iron Shirt had on his war bonnet; he hadn't worn it since the attack on Fort Parker. The morning sun was shining on the many colored feathers, creating a beautiful sight.

Peta came with her horse. She tried to get on, but was too short, so Peta with his strong arms placed her on the horse. He then mounted his horse and rode up beside her. The Indians were now all mounted and ready to ride, but no one moved. She saw many riders coming towards them and she wasn't sure what was going to happen. They also had their war paint on and were dressed in their best clothes. Were the Indians going to attack another fort?

Cynthia Ann watched the camp warriors stop and wave. Then Iron Shirt raised his lance into the air and his warriors fell in behind him. They lined up in the order of recognition of the acts they performed at Fort Parker. Iron Shirt, as their leader, carried high the lance with all the scalps tied on it for everyone to see. High Wolf and Peta rode behind Iron Shirt with her between them.

When Cynthia Ann rode over the next hill she could see the Indian tepee all lined up along creek. She heard the voices of women singing, then saw them coming towards them to greet the warriors. After the raiding party passed, the women singers fell to the rear of the parade.

She was scared because the camp members came outside the camp lining both sides of the warriors, shouting, yelling and dancing. On entering the camp, the warrior would go directly to his own tepee.

Peta stopped at his father's tepee and handed her over to his mother, Sikway. Sikway sent Iron Shirt's three other wives with her to bathe in the river. Ahtookoo, Iron Shirt's second wife, stood on the bank so she could oversee the bathing.

"Strip her clothes off!" she yelled. Cynthia Ann grabbed her dress at the top and was holding on to it for dear life. These women scared her; how she wished Peta had stayed to protect her from them. She held on to her dress, but her legs and Cona's legs, Iron Shirt's third wife, got tangled up and they both fell under the water. She came up coughing and spitting out water just as Habbe, Iron Shirt's fourth wife, jerked her dress off.

"Wash her with sand. That will clean and purify her," ordered Ahtookoo. The two women washed her with sand until her skin turned red. As she stumbled out of the water, she looked up and saw Peta standing high on the bank looking down at her. Her face reddened and she looked at the ground as Ahtookoo placed a soft deer skin robe around her. She looked back to where Peta was standing, but he was gone.

When she arrived back to the tepee, Sikway dressed her in a pure white buckskin. Habbe combed her blond hair with a brush made from the tail of a porcupine, then braided her hair tying the ends with white ribbons. Iron Shirt sat quietly outside the tepee waiting for the women to dress her.

Sikway led Cynthia Ann outside. Iron Shirt looked up at her. He couldn't remember when he had seen a more beautiful maiden. Her hair shone with the radiance of the sun. Iron Shirt took her hand and led her through the camp. It was to show the camp she was a virgin; also, she was his property, and no one was to touch or harm her in any way. After Iron Shirt showed her the camp, he took her to his mother, Gray Foot.

"Gray Foot, we are here," Iron Shirt yelled, because Gray Foot at her age was hard of hearing.

"So this is the one I'm to train to be the wife of Peta when she gets older."

"Yes! I have named her Naduah which means 'Someone Found'."

"Naduah is a good name and I will care for her as if she is my own. I will train her in the ways of our people and she will

make Peta a wife any chief can be proud of."

"All I ask is you teach her well, but also be firm and kind."

"I will, my son."

Cynthia Ann didn't understand what they were saying, but she knew they were talking about her. Gray Foot reached for her hand and led her into the tepee. Gray Foot sat down and pointed for Cynthia Ann to do the same. This was the beginning of her Comanche training which lasted until an hour before sundown. Gray foot pointed to Cynthia Ann and said "Naduah" in Comanche. She kept repeating until Cynthia Ann pointed to herself and said "Naduah."

* * *

Naduah and Gray Foot went to help the women and children gather wood for the Victory Dance. A scalp pole had been set with the scalps attached on the top. They lit the fire before dark. The singers, drummers, and older ones seated themselves near the pole. She and Gray Foot were sitting with the singers, and her eyes stopped on one scalp. It was her grandfather's. There at the top was Elder John's long gray scalp.

The drummers started drumming and were joined by the singers. The men were wearing their war bonnets with their faces painted red; the women were in their best dresses with their faces painted black. The men and women dancers formed lines facing each other and danced backward and forward, then formed a circle and danced around the scalp pole, while the watchers joined in the singing.

She was feeling the rhythm of the drums and was patting her knees in time with them. She hummed along because she couldn't remember the words. She didn't realize all the songs were different. They all sounded alike to her because of the same rhythm.

The rhythm of the singing and the loud chanting of the dancers reminded her of when her grandfather, Elder John, preached a congregation into a frenzy. She felt sad her grandfather was dead; she knew he was in heaven and a part of him was there with her as she looked to the top of the scalp pole.

Elder John always told her that he would die, and when he did she shouldn't feel sad, but feel happy for him instead because he would be walking with God. She wondered if Elder John was walking with God without any hair.

Chapter 7

TINNIN'S SETTLEMENT.

JUNE 1, 1836

James Parker walked to the road in front of Captain Carter's house. He saw a figure moving towards him and it looked familiar. He couldn't make out the man's features, but it was the way he walked. He quickly ran to meet him.

"Luther Plummer, how did you find us?"

"I have been following you ever since the attack on the fort. You sure did a good job of hiding your tracks. I finally just gave up and headed for Tinnin," Luther said.

"We arrived last night and the women and children are worn out."

"James, are my wife, Rachel, and son, James Platt, here with you?"

"No, I haven't seen them."

"Then they must have been taken as captives. James, what will I do?" Luther asked sadly.

"Maybe they are with the others."

"No, I don't think so. I was with the men when they saved Lucy and her children."

"Then they are all safe?"

"No, the Indians captured John and Cynthia Ann. James, how will we ever find them?"

"Captain Carter tells me that a Major Moody has available five hundred Rangers at his command. I will go and see him and ask him for a company of men."

"They have a seven day head start."

"Luther, we have to start someplace. Now, let's get you something to eat. I'll head for Major Moody's."

Leaving Luther at the Carter's with the survivors, he headed to Major Moody's. Finding the Major's cabin, he met a round-shouldered man with graying hair.

"Sir, are you Major Moody?"

"Yes, I am, and who do I have the pleasure of addressing?"

"I'm James Parker."

"James, I have heard of your hardship in leading your family here."

"Sir, I'm here to ask your help. One of my sons-in-laws arrived this morning and tells me that some of the families were taken captive by the Indians. I need a company of Rangers to go with me back to Fort Parker to find out how many were killed or captured. I'm penniless now because everything I own is back at the fort."

"I have good news for you. This very morning I received a report two companies of Rangers are returning home tomorrow. I will send word as soon as they arrive."

"I thank you for your kindness, and I'll wait until I hear from you," James said, shaking Major Moody's hand.

When James arrived back at Captain Carter's house, he found his other son-in-law, Levin Nixon. Nixon had helped the other group get settled at Fort Houston, and took one of the horses and rode south to Tinnin's Settlement. He then decided to look for James and his group. Nixon told them who was killed or captured at the fort. Mrs. Frost learned her husband, Samuel, and son, Robert, had been killed. James' family learned Rachel, James Platt Plummer, Cynthia Ann, John Parker, and Elizabeth Kellogg were all captives of the Indians.

The next day he waited for word from Major Moody, but no word came. That evening, Dickens, Plummer, and Nixon came to him.

"We have decided when the Rangers arrive we and our families will travel part way back with you, but we will turn east on the trail for Fort Houston," Nixon said, not looking at James.

"Those women and children are in no shape to make the walk back to Fort Houston. God, man, they almost died coming here. It will be weeks before they can make that trip."

"I have some money, and Granny sent some for the survivors, if I found any," Nixon replied, handing James a bag.

It was two days later when James received a message from Major Moody. The message said the Rangers had been called back to Washington on the Brazos. There were rumors that Santa Anna Army was returning to Texas. The Rangers were being held ready to meet the army.

It was then Nixon, Plummer, and Dickens decided to go to Fort Houston. Nixon purchased two horses and supplies for the trip. The women and children could take turns riding on the three horses. They were all ready to leave the next morning. James and his family were there saying their good-byes. Nixon walked over to James and asked, "James, are you sure you won't come with us?"

"I'm not sure if Martha is strong enough to make the trip, so we are moving to Grimes just south of here instead. With the Rangers gone, Tinnin is just like Fort Parker, open to an Indian attack."

"James, as soon as we get these people back to Fort Houston and Granny gets better, Sarah and I will catch up with you and Martha."

"Wait until we get settled and I will send you word." The group moved away, waving at each other.

James purchased a horse and some supplies because Martha was still very frail after the trip from Fort Parker. The next day, he thanked the Carters for the care they had provided for his family. He loaded the few supplies. He then helped Martha, Francis Marion, four years old, and Patsy, eight months old, onto the horse. He walked ahead leading the horse, stopping often because of Martha's weakened condition. It took them fivedays to make the thirty mile journey to Grimes.

James left Martha and the children in the shade of a large large oak tree after they arrived in Grimes. He walked into the Settlement when he saw a well close by and headed for it. As he approached the well a man called out to him, "There is nothing as good as a cool drink of water after a day on the hot trail. Where are you from, friend?"

"I'm James Parker from Fort Parker. We have just come from Tinnin."

"I am known as Judge Grimes. I heard that you were in Tinnin and what a time you had getting there with the women and children. If there is anything I can do for you, just let me know."

"Well, sir, there is. We need a place to live."

"I know just the place. It's about a mile on down the road. You'll find it on the left-hand side of the road. The house looks like it has a shed built onto it. The Dunman family is living in the house, but they let other people live in the shed part."

"Thank you, but there is also something else. I would like to raise a company of men, if it's possible, and go back to Fort Parker to see what's left."

"I can't guarantee anything, but I will ask around. You come to see me in a couple of days.""

"Sir, I feel grateful for your kindness to me and my family."

James filled his water bag and left the Judge. They had no trouble finding the house that the Judge had described. The shed part of the house was a bare room with a dirt floor. After James told Dunman who he was, they were happy to let James and his family live there. James set to work making the beds. He cut four small trees each containing a fork in the top. After cutting the poles for length, he drove the four poles into the ground to make the ends of the beds, then he placed poles in the forks. After finding some slab boards, he laid them on the poles and strewed straw on top of the boards for a pallet. When he had finished, Martha laid down on the new bed. It was the first bed she had been in for more than three weeks.

With the help of Judge Grimes, James raised a company of thirteen men to go with him back to Fort Parker. They were to leave the next day. That evening, his family came down with the measles. Since he had arranged to leave the next day, he asked Dr. Adams, and his new landlord to care for his family while he was away.

He and his company arrived back at Fort Parker on the 19th of June, one month after the attack. He couldn't find any tracks to indicate which way the Indians had left; too much time had elapsed. What little trail the Indians left had vanished completely. The fort and cabins were still standing, but the crops were destroyed and the horses had been stolen.

James felt he should return to Grimes and to his sick family. The company rounded up what cattle they could and headed back to Grimes.

He arrived back in Grimes and found his wife near death. Dr. Adams, who had been attending Martha, told him that she would die. He asked the doctor if he could administer the medicines to her and the children. He believed Martha's sickness was more in her head than in her body. Martha's body, lying on the straw pallet, had been reduced to skin and bones. James' presence gave her hope.

"Martha, if you will just get well, I promise, I will search for Rachel, James Platt, Elizabeth, Cynthia Ann, and John. I will not rest until they are found."

"You will do this for me, James?"

"Yes, but I can't leave you in this condition."

He took care of Martha for seven days. He didn't know if it was his care or the promise he made to find the captives, but with their mother getting well, the children improved also. He felt his family was well enough to travel and moved them further away from the frontier. He sold the cattle and they moved fifty miles south into Austin's colony of the First Three Hundred. He purchased a tract of land from Benson Risinghover where he built a cabin for his family.

Chapter 8

NOCONIS CAMP ON THE PEASE RIVER.

JUNE 25, 1836

Iron Shirt decided to go to his mother's tepee to see how Naduah was adjusting to The People's ways. When he arrived the tent was empty. He walked on towards the river and met Naduah loaded down with sticks. Behind her was Gray Foot with a big smile on her face, "I'll say one thing for her, she is a worker and will do well. She has the ability and is eager to learn."

"I knew she would. I watched her all the time on the trail until I brought her to you."

"I will need to dry more meat because she eats like a horse."

"That's another reason I came. In the morning I'm sending Peta with others on a buffalo hunt. I sent runners out yesterday. They have returned telling me a small herd of buffalo are close by. Peta will now be responsible not only for his own tepee, but also for you and Naduah."

"We will prepare more drying racks this afternoon," said Gray Foot with a big smile.

* * *

Naduah had placed her load of wood on the wood pile and she listened to them talk. The only words she understood were her name, Peta, and meat. Life with The People wasn't so much different. Gray Foot reminded her of Granny, soft spoken, and always with a smile on her brown wrinkled and kind-looking face. She did the same work here as at the fort of carrying water and firewood. The food was different though, a diet of cooked meat. How she wished she could have a piece of her mother's fresh baked bread. But she liked the tepee better than her cabin at the fort. The small fire in the center kept the tepee warm all night. At night they burned buffalo chips because chips burn longer. Her bed here was built up only a foot off the ground. At the fort she slept in the top bunk with John sleeping in the bunk below.

As Iron Shirt walked away she couldn't help thinking about Peta. He was just like Iron Shirt; they both had a hard mean look with eyes that bore holes into you.

She followed Gray Foot along the river to where the willows grew. She watched Gray Foot cut a willow over an inch in diameter. Gray Foot handed her the crude axes and motioned for her to cut more. As she cut the willows down, Gray Foot trimmed. It wasn't long until they had all the poles needed to make more drying racks.

She was learning the Comanche's language because Gray Foot never stopped teaching her. Even as they walked back, she stopped and pointed out an object and said its name. She was repeating it in Comanche and in English. Gray Foot was learning a few English words while she was learning Comanche.

* * *

Iron Shirt sent word for Peta to come to his tepee. Iron Shirt was sitting facing the opening when Cona announced him. Peta entered and sat opposite the fire facing his father.

"Peta, I'm talking today not only as your Chief, but also your father. High Wolf is leading a buffalo hunt in the morning. You will go with him since I must stay here. You are responsible for our family hunt. Naduah is your captive. She is too young for bedding. I have placed her under my protection and have let Gray Foot teach her our ways. Do you understand why I did this?"

"When do I get her?"

"You both have to earn that right. It is something that I will not give you and her. She will have to learn the ways of The People. While she is learning, you will provide for her and Gray Foot. You are also to give her a horse, and teach her to ride as well as any warrior."

"How can I do this without becoming the laughing stock of the band?"

"Most of the ones laughing are jealous; they're not the ones teaching her."

"I'll try."

"You'll not only try, but you will do it. If you run into any problems, come to me and we, together, will work it out."

* * *

Peta, downhearted, left the tepee, but when he was around Naduah, she excited him. It was the way she looked at him and smiled, even when things weren't going well. Iron Shirt must think she was special to give her this kind of treatment. Naduah was never abused to make her bend to the ways of The People.

He walked through the camp deep in thought, not realizing where he was going. Before he knew it, he was standing in front of Gray Foot's tepee. Her voice startled him, "It is good you have come to see me."

"Iron Shirt said I'm to give Naduah a horse and teach her to ride."

"That's fine, but where is the horse?"

"I-I-thought maybe Naduah would like to pick out her own horse," he answered, with a stutter in his voice.

"Why don't you ask her? She is there beside the tepee finishing rawhiding the drying rack together."

His face turned all colors of red. He started to say something, but thought better of it. Gray Foot could always get to him, for she had been doing so since he was a little boy. Walking around the tepee Naduah's eyes met his but she looked away quickly. He cleared his throat, "Iron Shirt said I am to give you a horse. I thought that you would like to pick one out for yourself."

Naduah's face went blank. What was he talking about? Gray Foot started laughing, "Here, you both want to talk to each other and can't. I'll go with you and help you pick out a horse for her," Gray Foot said, motioning Naduah to follow them.

* * *

Peta led the way to where the horses were grazing. He nodded to the horse herder with a smile. He walked slowly through the herd and saw his favorite horse, Star, running to meet him. He stopped and gently rubbed Star's head and neck. He walked on with Star following him, looking for a small brown mare for Naduah.

He found the small brown mare he was looking for. He turned. There was Star and Gray Foot, but no Naduah. Then he saw her rubbing and loving a pinto horse.

It was Paint, his second best horse next to Star. There was no way in the world she could ride him. Peta tried to explain all this to Gray Foot. Gray Foot, talking in mixed Comanche and broken English, pointed to the brown mare. Naduah was shaking her head "no" and kept pointing to the pinto.

* * *

Naduah could tell that Peta was losing his patience. She turned to the pinto, grabbed a hand full of mane and was on his back racing away from the herd. Peta mounted Star and raced after her. She saw him coming; therefore, she turned the pinto around quickly and headed straight at him. She wasn't going to give Peta the chance to grab her off the pinto like he did at the fort. She learned how to use her knees to guide and control an Indian horse on the long ride from Fort Parker.

She was urging the pinto on. He had laid his ears back and was running for all he had. She kept him headed straight for Peta and they were closing fast. She never batted an eye, but stared straight ahead. Peta turned Star to his right. She turned the pinto the same. The only thought in Peta's mind was if anything happened to this crazy girl, Iron Shirt would skin him alive. He turned more to the right to get away from her. She rode past him and headed for Gray Foot where she slid the pinto to a stop and dismounted gracefully. She rubbed the horse and gave him a big hug. Peta rode up, jumped off Star, and started yelling and screaming. She turned her back on him and looked at Gray Foot, who was holding her stomach because she was laughing so hard.

"Tell her that she can't have Paint."

"Do you want me to tell Iron Shirt what happened here?"

Peta answered reluctantly, "She can have Paint."

She led Paint away from the herd to where there was tall grass. After pulling the grass she gave Paint a rub down. She had seen the warriors do this while getting ready for the parade when they first brought her to the camp. Paint liked having his neck and back rubbed. When she was finished rubbing Paint down, she walked back towards Gray Foot and Peta. Paint followed her as if she were leading him.

Walking right up to Peta, looking as mean as she could, she patted her chest and pointed to Paint, "My horse."

Peta's face, flushing with hostility, answered angrily, "Naduah's horse."

She looked at Gray Foot who nodded her head "Yes." She turned, gave Paint a hug, and walked towards the tepee, followed by Gray Foot. Peta, shrugging his shoulders, plodded along behind. Naduah knew she had won a great victory over Peta, but she also knew he would get even with her later because he wasn't one to be defeated so easily. At the tepee she picked up a buffalo paunch and headed for the spring. They needed water and she wanted to get away from Peta quickly.

Peta stood watching her walk away. He liked her, but he also hated her. As a captive, she always seemed to get her own way. Confused, Peta hurried to Iron Shirt's tepee. Peta barged in the tepee not waiting to be announced. Iron Shirt looked at him with surprise, but motioned him to sit.

"Why do you look like you lost your best friend?"

"Naduah has nerves of steel. She can ride, and she selected my best horse!" Peta yelled.

"Calm down and tell me what happened."

Peta related what happened between him and Naduah in the selection of Paint. Iron Shirt was having a hard time keeping from laughing. His wives rushed out of the tepee so they couldn't hear them laughing.

"It sounds to me she knows horses or the Great Spirit is guiding her. You made a mistake by not selecting a horse and taking it to her. Now you must live with what has been done because you gave her the horse. There is no way you can take it back. It's hers."

"What if something happens to Star?"

"You had better check your herd or trade for a good horse. You say she can ride but that's not good enough. She must be able to ride as well as you did when you were her age."

"But she is a girl!"

"So was your mother once. She could out ride me until you were born. Naduah is still yours to train after the buffalo hunt. I expect you to take her riding and work with her."

"I'll do as you say, but she is different."

"I hope she is, because that's the new blood The People need."

Peta left feeling worse than before he had talked to Iron Shirt. He needed to get his equipment ready for the hunt. The hunting party would be leaving before dawn. Now, not only did he have to feed her, but she had also taken his good horse. He wasn't sure if he went on another raid he would choose to take another captive. Stealing horses was much easier.

* * *

Naduah carried the water and picked up firewood. She was every place at once. When she had finished, she ran to Gray Foot. With her blue eyes shining she bragged, "See Paint."

Gray Foot laughed to herself as she said, "Yes," in Comanche. She followed Naduah, watching her run down the path. The horses raised their heads as she entered the grazing area. The horse herder just smiled because he had witnessed the morning events. Paint raised his head, neighed, and ran to meet Naduah. She hugged and patting him all over. Gray Foot had never seen a horse show affection for a person like Paint.

Chapter 9

THE HEADWATERS OF THE ARKANSAS RIVER IN COLORADO.
JULY 15,1836

Rachel Plummer, a captive of the Yamparikas Comanche led by Chief Howes, had traveled 45 days after being separated from her son, James Platt. She had arrived at what the Yamparikas Comanche call their home, Snow Mountain. Chief Howes gave her to Yellow Moon because he was the one who captured her.

She was traded by Yellow Moon to Loud Talker for ten tanned buffalo hides and four horses. Rachel found out Loud Talker was now too old to hunt and his wife, Elk Woman, was well up in years. Their only son was killed in a raid into Mexico. All they had left was a lazy daughter named Sleepy One. They lived by tanning buffalo hides for the other members of the band. Loud Talker received one hide for every five hides they tanned. He traded his hides for meat and other supplies. Sleepy One started Rachel working at scraping a hide. She started thinking about James Platt and wondering where he was and how he was being treated. She didn't realize she had slowed down scraping the hide until Sleepy One hit her across the back with a stick. She returned to work, and learned to keep an eye out for Sleepy One. Her thoughts returned to all the things that had happened to her in the past month and a half.

How she stood the unbearable treatment of the trip she didn't know. Now, just thinking about it made her sick. Her head had healed where she had been hit on the head with a hoe, but her mind and soul would never be the same. The first night was the worst when they stripped her of her clothes. She lost count of how many men had her before she passed out.

While traveling without her clothes she became blistered from the sun. The Indians on the trail had named her Red Skin because her skin looked like it was on fire. Yellow Moon smeared her with mud every morning before taking to the trail. It was when they crossed the Red River she found a black oily pool. She bathed her whole body in it and the burns felt much better. Before leaving, she took her bandanna from her head and filled it. She used it to wipe down her burns for the next two days. The rag lost its oily feeling, but her burns were better.

Yellow Moon gave her a shirt to wear for the rest of the trip but she still had scars which hadn't healed completely. She learned much of the Comanche language while they were traveling. She had learned it was better to just give in than to try to fight back.

She saw out of the corner of her eye that Elk Woman was heading in her direction. She started chipping away on the hide faster with the adze made from steel cutting edge bound with rawhide to the handle of an elk horn. Elk Woman screamed, "No, no," jerking the scraper from her hand. Elk Woman then started chopping with small even strokes removing blood, fat, and flesh. She turned and handed the scraper back to her. Elk Woman then reached down and rubbed the area that she had cleaned. She took her hand and rubbed it across the area. She then turned to her and held her thumb apart from her index finger and waved it back and forth in her face.

She nodded, waved her thumb and index finger back at her and rubbed the skin. Elk Woman smiled and nodded her head 'yes' and walked away. She went back to scraping the hide. Now she knew it is supposed to be clean, smooth, and all the same thickness. She could hear Elk Woman yelling at Sleepy One who was staking hide for her to clean. Sleepy One was to help her scrape the hides, but she never scraped more than two hides a day. Her quota was ten and Sleepy was suppose to stake fifteen and lay the clean hides out in the sun to cure. The sun would cure and bleach the hide, but they needed wetting down occasionally. Just before dark, Elk Woman came to look at the cleaned hides to see if they needed wetting down. If they did, she had to carry the water from the stream and do it.

Rachel's other duty was to watch the horse herd at night. High up on the mountain side the nights were cold. Elk Woman had given her one of Sleepy One's old dresses which was too large for her as Sleepy One was a big woman. She altered thebuckskin dress while she watched the horses at night. The dress helped protect her from the cold. She sat with her legs and feet covered since she had no shoes.

She believed Elk Woman knew that she was doing most of Sleepy One's hides, but together they were turning out fifteen hides a day. This was giving them three hides a day to sell or trade to the traders. She heard Loud Taker telling Elk Woman that their lives were better now for the first time since they had lost their sons.

The days were long for her, scraping hides all day and taking care of the horses all night. She wasn't sure if she wanted her child to be born into this Indian world. The Yamparikas are a cruel tribe. They want slaves to do their work and also for their sexual pleasure. They had no interest in having mixed-blood or white-blooded children. When the traders came, maybe they would trade her. She had heard that Comancheros traders purchased Mrs. Harris before she arrived.

She prayed every day the traders would come. It was the only thing that kept her going. Sleepy One was making her work harder and beating her more each day. Her only hope of living was with the traders. She was already cleaning fifteen hides a day, so Elk Woman raised the quota to twenty. Sleepy One was only cleaning two or three hides a day. Elk Woman was well pleased when she inspected her hides at the end of the day.

If only she didn't have to care for the horses. She was so tired. The night had been quiet and she had slept more than usual. She just finished her third hide when the Comancheros traders came into camp. They traded all over the camp before they came to Loud Talker's tepee. The traders had most of their carts loaded down with hides, but still had goods to trade. It was the first time she had ever seen a Comancheros who was a cross between a Mexican and an Indian. There were more than twenty in the Comancheros party.

She noticed one man was white with a dark tan, and he stood out with his blond hair and blue eyes. He watched her scrape the hide while the others traded with Loud Talker for his hides. When Loud Talker finished trading, the white man approached Loud Talker, "How much for the woman?"

"She's not for trade."

"I will trade new guns, shot, and powder for her."

"She's not for trade."

"I also will trade you tobacco, whiskey, and kettles."

"She's not for trade."

By now, she could understand Comanche. Her hopes and dreams were now in the hands of a man she didn't even know. Her life with him couldn't be any worse than it was here. Her new baby might still get a chance to grow up.

"I will throw in ten packages of metal arrowheads, both kinds, hunting and warring arrowheads. They alone are worth ten hides."

"She's not for trade."

The white man shook his head turned and walked away. She almost fainted falling forward on the hide. Why had God forsaken her? If she had ever needed his help, it was now. She wasn't sure she could take too much more of this cruel and unjust treatment. She wished they would just kill her because life was so unbearable. Straightening up off the hide, she saw the white man returning to speak to Loud Talker. This gave her new strength and hope. Maybe he could buy her. She dried her eyes by squeezing them tightly together. Still the tears ran down her face which she wiped on her shirt as she scraped the hide.

"Loud Talker, if you ever want to trade that white woman, bring her to me. I will give you more than anyone else," he said as he turned, gave her a smile, and mounted his horse riding away. She watched as he and the Comancheros with their heavy wooden ox carts moved away from the camp.

Sleepy One wasn't keeping the hides ahead of her covered with moistened wood ash which neutralized the fatty greasy surface. The hides were a lot easier to scrape and left a smoother surface when the ash was used. She stopped scraping and started spreading the ash. Elk Woman saw she was putting the ash on the hides and she hurried over to her.

"You keep scraping. I will see that Sleepy One puts the ash on ahead of you," she said and headed for Sleepy One.

She knew she was in trouble because Sleepy One would get even with her, even though it wasn't her fault. Elk Woman was yelling at Sleepy One and was using words that she had never heard before. The only thing she recognized was the tone of her voice. She scraped harder and faster on the hide because she didn't want Elk Woman mad at her. Sleepy One would be mad at her for the rest of the day.

It was late in the afternoon and she had forgotten about Sleepy One being mad at her. She had lost all track where Sleepy One was, and before she knew it, Sleepy One hit her across the back, knocking her flat on the hide. She could hardly get her breath; the pain in her back was killing her, but she pushed herself up. Turning over on her back, she stared hard at Sleepy One who was ready to hit her again. She still had the scraping tool in her hand and the look on her face was a determined one. This stopped Sleepy One and she walked away. She was hurt but felt good inside because Sleepy One had backed down. The next time Sleepy One hit her, she was going to fight back.

She took a buffalo robe with her when she went to herd the horses. She spread the robe on the ground, covered up with it, and tried to sleep. If they were going to beat her when she worked hard, she wondered, how much worse could it get? She dreamed the white Trader had traded for her and she was back with white people again. Would they accept her, or would she be looked on as white trash? She woke up with a feeling that

God was punishing her. If she had been a better Person, none of this would have happened.

Her feet felt like they were frozen. The air had turned cold in the night; there was frost on the grass and she could see her breath. She felt tired, not knowing how long she had slept. The horses were gone! She jumped to her feet and ran in a large circle around the area. Out of breath, she almost gave up when she saw where they had knocked the frost off the grass. She followed the trail for a quarter of a mile before she found the horses. The horses were all right, munching on the tall grass. She rounded the horses up and drove them back to the pasture. The sun was now up and the horse herder came to relieve her.

Elk Woman, who was cooking a piece of meat over the fire offered her a piece. She ate the meat quickly and started scraping hides. She had one hide finished before Sleepy One came out of the tepee. Elk Woman yelled at Sleepy One trying to get her to work, but Sleepy One moved at her normal slow speed. She wondered how long it would be before the trader returned. She quickly put the thoughts out of her mind because there was no use in getting her hopes up.

Chapter 10

Naduah was scraping a buffalo hide when she heard the camp crier riding through the camp. She couldn't make out all the words, but it had something to do with the camp. Gray Foot stepped outside the tepee and listened to him. "What does he say about the camp?" she asked with a puzzled look.

"He said we are moving in the morning. There will be good water, shade, and buffalo."

"Why are we moving?"

"We have been here a long time and the camp is dirty. We are moving to a clean camp. Come, we must start packing. The first one there gets the best camp sites."

She followed Gray Foot into the tepee and pulled packs out from under the beds. Gray Foot handed one of the bags to her and started throwing personal items on the bed. "Fill the packs as full as you can get them," Gray Foot said, not even looking around.

She was busy packing and repacking until she had packed four buffalo packs. The bags contained ornaments, horn spoons, wooden bowls, and extra clothing. Gray foot was packing dried meat into two bags. She then helped Gray Foot take down the beds.

"What are we going to sleep on tonight?"

"We will sleep on buffalo hide and cover up with buffalo robes," Gray Foot said as she poured water on the fire. "Now you go and fill the bag with fresh water for the trip."

When she returned she found Iron Shirt's wife, Habbe, talking to Gray Foot.

"Come, we will show you your job on moving day."

She followed Gray Foot and Habbe into the tepee. Gray foot squatted down a little to let Habbe place her foot on her thigh. Habbe

49

looked like a cat standing on Gray Foot's shoulder. Habbe started removing the wooden skewers that fastened the covering at the top. The wooden skewers were small sticks sharpened on one end. After Habbe removed the top skewers, she removed the skewers from the front of the tepee that held the seams together. The buffalo hide slid to the ground. Together, they pulled the covering away from the tepee and folded it up.

She was worn out and glad when the sun hid itself, and laid down on the hide and was asleep before she knew it. Gray Foot stood smiling down at her and covered her with a robe. She slept soundly all night. She couldn't believe it was already morning. Gray Foot was shaking her trying to wake her up.

"Come. We must get our horses now," Gray Foot turned and hurried away.

She caught up with Gray Foot as she entered the horses' pasture. She saw Paint and he ran to her. Gray Foot carried three short braided horse hair ropes. Gray Foot handed one to Naduah, "Place this around his neck and follow me."

She had a hard time keeping up. Gray Foot moved through the herd quickly and placed a rope around the neck of a brown mare. Gray Foot handed the end of the rope to her and told her to take them to the tepee. She tied the horses to a small tree behind the tepee. She was walking around the tepee when Gray Foot arrived with a large black mare.

* * *

Gray Foot tied the mare to a stake in front of the tepee. She placed a special saddle on the black mare, and with Naduah's help tied the tepee poles to both sides of the mare. Together, they placed the tepee covering on the travois, tying it down with rawhide. She put two bags on her horse and placed two on Paint. The rest of the bags she placed and tied on the travois.

She mounted the brown mare and led the black mare. Naduah swung on Paint and rode along side of Gray Foot. Naduah thought they were the first to leave camp, but there were many moving ahead.

"Why are there still tepee standing?" Naduah asked, looking around the camp.

"Some of them will join the band later. Others will stay for a while or join another band," she replied, urging the mare to pick up the pace.

This puzzled Naduah, but she rode silently. It wasn't long until they reached the Red River. The Indians were moving across in single file.

"You keep Paint behind the black mare," she said.

* * *

Naduah saw Peta on the other side watching as Naduah got to the river. Paint wouldn't enter the water. He kept turning into circles. She saw Peta laughing. She was going to show him. When Paint turned away, she rode him a short distance, turned him around, and ran him straight for the river. Peta saw what she was doing and jumped Star into the river.

The strong currents were pushing her downstream towards the shallows that were nothing but quick sand. Peta pushed Star for all the horse had as she and Paint were getting closer to the shallows. Peta turned Star as he grabbed the bridles rein from Naduah's hand. The strength of Peta pulling on Paint's rein and the will of Paint to follow Star turned Paint upstream into the current. He wasn't swimming, just fighting the water

Peta knew how much Paint hated the water, but he was a complete horse on land. Peta realized something needed to be done, or they would end up in the quick sand. He pushed himself backwards off Star, grabbing Naduah with his right hand, and pulled her off Paint. With his left hand, he grabbed hold of Star's tail and hung on for dear life.

Star, now relieved of the weight on his back, swam up stream easily, pulling Peta and her behind. She looked over her shoulder and saw Paint was following. When Star was on dry land, Peta let go of his tail. Getting to his feet quickly, he dragged her up on dry land. The people who lined the river banks cheered. Coughing, gagging, and spitting up water from her mouth, she thought she had swallowed half of the water in the river. Gray Foot ran to her, "Are you all right? We thought you were a goner. You were almost in the quick sand."

Paint came out of the water with Star. They were standing beside Peta. "I told you Paint was too much horse for you." He turned and walked away with Star following.

She turned and rubbed Paint gently, "He just doesn't like water."

"You made your mistake by jumping him straight into the river. Next time jump him in towards the current. You always head upstream into the current because it will carry you down," Gray Foot said, with a smile on her face.

"When we get to the new camp, I'll see he loves water."

"Come along; we are losing our place in line."

She mounted Paint. As her stomach felt queasy from swallowing the river's salty mineral water, she didn't feel well. She was mad at herself because Peta had to help her cross the river. The sun was hot and the dust from the ones in front settled on her wet body and clothes.

She was glad when they stopped to camp early in the afternoon. They made camp at a big spring near the Prairie Dog Fork of the Red River. She helped Gray Foot unpack the travois and headed for the river, and waded right into the river with her clothes on. She washed herself and her hair that had become matted from the dust, and tasted the water. It wasn't bitter like the Red.

Returning to where Gray Foot had unloaded for their one night camp, "Is there quicksand in this river?"

"No, why do you ask?" Gray Foot stood with a puzzled look on her face.

"Then now would be a good time to teach Paint to like water while he is tired."

"Not without Peta, because you have a knack for getting yourself into trouble."

"He doesn't like me and is still mad at me because of Paint."

"He likes you, but you took his good horse. You don't ride him without one of us with you."

"Then you go with me."

"No, you find Peta because I'm too tired."

"OK, but he will not go; I know he won't."

"One of the first things you need to learn is to think more positive."

"OK," and with her head down started through the camp looking for Peta.

She saw Peta was talking to Little Foot and some other braves when he caught a glimpse of Naduah coming towards him.

Little Foot started smiling, "There's the little gal that made you a hero today. I think it's time we all leave so she can thank you without us embarrassing her."

Peta's face turned red. This was all he needed, but Iron Shirt had made it plain that he, alone, was responsible for her. Naduah walked right up to him. Looking at the ground she said, "I want to ride Paint into the river."

"Well, go ahead. He's your horse now."

"Gray Foot said you have to ride with me."

"I'm tired, Star is tired, Paint is tired, and you should be tired."

"If Paint is tired, maybe he will enter the water."

"Paint almost drowned when he was young while crossing the Red River. He was swept away in the changing currents. It was all Little Foot and I could do to save him."

"Can you make him enter the water?"

"Yes, he is afraid of me, but he's in love with you."

"Will you help me?" She smiled and looked up into his face.

"Since you asked like that, yes. You go and pick up your bridle, and I will meet you where the horses are grazing."

She hurried to get her bridle and ran to where the horses were grazing. Paint saw her and only moved slowly towards her. She rubbed him well then placed the lip bridle on him. She mounted Paint and saw Peta heading towards her.

Peta stopped short of the river and moved Star close to Paint. He had brought a rope he tied around Paint's neck. "Now, try to enter him towards the upstream current."

She pushed Paint towards the water, but he wouldn't enter. The harder she tried the more he resisted. Paint stayed on the bank and was just moving along it. She was pulling hard on his bridle and applying knee pressure. Peta and Star had entered the river. Peta had fastened a rope band around Star's chest; before he entered the river he tied the end of the rope around Paint's neck. Without warning, Peta turned Star and jerked Paint into the river.

She was as surprised as Paint and almost fell off but caught herself. Paint started to fight the water. He wasn't trying to swim. She relaxed allowing Paint to have his head, and was amazed how he quit fighting the river and started swimming. Peta kept Star along side, but behind them. Paint swam straight to the opposite bank. Peta removed the rope from around Paint's neck, "Now, try him again."

She rode Paint a short distance away from the river, and turned him back to the river where Peta sat on Star. When Paint reached the water's edge, he stopped abruptly and almost threw her over his head into the river. After she recovered herself, Peta slapped Paint on the rear with his rope. This scared Paint as much as it hurt. He jumped into the water and swam across the river.

Peta sat on the other bank trying not to laugh, but he couldn't help himself. She wasn't pleased; he almost caused her to be thrown off, but

Paint did cross. She headed Paint back across the river. He hesitated at the water's edge, pranced a little and crossed.

"Now that he will cross the river, may we quit?"

"No, I would like to cross the river and ride through the field of wild flowers. They look so beautiful. Please, can't we?" she asked, smiling at him.

Peta couldn't resist the smile and her searching blue eyes. Before he realized it, he said, "Yes.! "

She started Paint towards the river, but he stopped at the water's edge. Peta hit him hard on the rump. He entered the water switching his tail; she didn't realized what Peta had done to Paint. She thought he entered on his own. While she rode through the area of wild flowers, Peta sat watching her ride around the blue, yellow, lavender, pink, red, and white wild colors.

She stopped, jumped off Paint, and started picking flowers. Peta laughed. No Indian girl would pick flowers. They would be picking edible plants. Iron Shirt could be right. Maybe this white girl was special. She jumped on Paint holding her wild flower bouquet and rode beside Peta.

"Why did you pick the wild flowers?"

"Because they are so pretty and they smell so good. I know that Gray Foot will love them."

"Are you ready to return to camp now?"

"Yes," she said while heading Paint back towards the river. This time Paint didn't stop at the water's edge, but ploughed off into the water and swam across. They turned their horses loose to graze with the rest of the horses. She gave the horse herder a big smile as they were leaving. Peta was unhappy at the way she looked at the herder, but he didn't say anything. The sun was now going down behind the mountains. A sunset of red and gold streaks mixed with white clouds marked the blue sky. As they entered their temporary camp, Peta went his way and she went hers.

"Thanks for helping me with Paint," she said, looking down at her bouquet.

Chapter 11

NACOGDOCHES, TEXAS.

AUGUST 20, 1836

After James built a cabin for his family and had taken care of their needs, he left them to fulfill his promise to Martha to find the captives. He headed to Nacogdoches where he hoped to find Sam Houston for help and authorization in raising a company of men. As he was riding, his mind wondered back to his last talk with Houston, who had disagreed with him about raising a company. Houston believed sending a company of Rangers against the Comanche was the worst thing that could be done. Houston felt the only way the captives could get their release was by treaty or ransom. James believed that Houston was wrong. The only way a treaty would work was to whip the Comanche and whip them good. After talking over his plan with Colonel Robbins and Colonel Sparks about what the three thought was feasible, they needed Houston's approval. It was his job to sell the plan to Houston. Since Houston had recovered from his wounds he received at the Battle of San Jacinto, he was now at his home in Nacogdoches.

A little after noon James dismounted in front of the trading post. He was tying his horse with his back to the trading post when he heard a voice, "Aren't you James Parker?"

Turning around he saw a man sitting in the shade. The man was wearing buckskins and had a long black beard. He knew the face, but couldn't put a name to it.

"Yes, I'm James Parker. May I inquire your name, sir?"

"I'm Bill Miligan. I saw you when I was a Ranger with your brother, Silas. We never met personally, but I was told who you were. I was sorry to hear about Fort Parker for your people had a good fort there. It's too bad about the captives."

"I came here to try and get Houston to help in getting the captives back."

"Say, would Mrs. Kellogg be one of them?"

"Do you know something about her?"

"Well, I was a talking to this Delaware Indian yesterday morning. He told me that his band traded for this white woman named Kellogg from the Caddo."

"Are you sure that it's Kellogg? How can I find her?"

"If you will buy me some tobacco, I will take you there. The Delaware are friendly Indians, but they have to be handled carefully. If you were to make the wrong move, you would never see her again."

"I don't have much money on me, but I will buy you tobacco if you will take me and help negotiate her release."

"You got yourself a deal."

He bought Bill his tobacco. They mounted and rode northwest for two hours. Bill stopped under the shade of a tree. "When we get inside the camp I want you to keep your mouth shut. If it's your Kellogg, just nod your head."

"Can't I talk to her?"

"No, 'cause we need to make them believe that we want just a white woman, any white woman."

"Then how will we get her back?"

"You leave that to me. I will try and negotiate a price."

He rode the rest of the way in silence because he knew that here he had no control. They were met by the young children running along side of their horses yelling and screaming. Bill rode on through the camp until he saw the Indian that he had talked to the day before.

Bill dismounted and talked to the Indian, then handed the reins of his horse to James and quietly said with a stern look on his face, "Stay here."

He noticed that the children had left him and the rest of the Indians were going about their own business. He sat there in the hot sun and wished that Bill had left him in the shade. Out of the corner of his eye he saw Bill coming with a woman and four Indian men. He looked hard at the woman. It took him a long time to visualize that she was even white. She was dressed in buckskin; her face was dark brown. He looked into her eyes haunted by inner pain.

He was speechless. The woman was Elizabeth. She stood there looking down at the ground. He heard a voice far away say something.

"James! I ask you, will this woman be alright?" Bill's stern voice snapped him out of his trance. He slowly nodded his head 'yes'. He could hear Bill talking to the Indians, but he kept his eyes fixed on Elizabeth. The Indians turned away, taking Elizabeth with them. He was still dazed until Bill jerked his horse's rein out of James' hand.

"Come on, let's get out of here."

"But ...."

"We will talk later-right now we ride."

They were half way back to the Post before Bill pulled into a cottonwood grove. Taking a big chew of tobacco, Bill said, "The Delaware traded the Caddo for her and gave them one hundred fifty dollars in goods for her. They are willing to trade her for that amount as they don't keep captives."

"I don't have that much money."

"James, if what I hear about you is true, you will get the money."

He rode silently the rest of the way to the Trading Post. Bill dismounted. Tying his horse he looked up and saw James riding away. "'That James Parker is a funny one," he said to his horse and entered the trading post.

James went straight to the home of Sam Houston where he found him sitting under a tree writing on an old table.

"Good evening, Mr. Houston. I carry good news. Elizabeth Kellogg has been traded to the Delaware Indians. They are willing to trade her for two hundred and fifty dollars which I don't have."

"Have you seen her?"

"Yes, this afternoon."

"Leave the trade to me. In the morning, I will go and see Chief Jim Ned who is one of biggest Indian traders in this area."

"I will wait at the trading post until I hear from you."

* * *

Early the next morning Sam Houston saddled his horse and a mare for Elizabeth, then rode to where Chief Jim Ned was camped. He had ridden around the trading post so that James wouldn't follow. He had no real proof but heard rumors that James traded horses with the Indians and paid them in counterfeit money. The Indians took revenge by attacking Fort Parker.

After going through the ceremonial ritual, brought up the subject of a white captive.

"I hear you traded for a white captive from the Caddo," he said with a firm look on his face.

"Yes, we traded."

"I would like to trade for her and return her to her family."

"I traded the Caddo one hundred and fifty dollars of goods for her, but I will let you have her for that amount. The same as I told the men that were here yesterday."

"You offered to trade her for that yesterday?"

"Yes."

His face changed to a look of concern. "I will have the Trading Post give you a credit for one hundred and fifty dollars worth of goods for the woman."

"My friend, let's shake on the deal and we'll go get the woman."

Houston followed Ned to a hut where he called out, "Bring the white woman out."

An Indian woman came out followed by a white woman and by younger girl who was giggling. The white woman was clean with hair combed and she wore white clothes.

"Are you Elizabeth Kellogg?" Houston asked, and watched as she nodded her head 'yes'.

"This mare is for you," he said, helping her onto the mare.

They rode for almost a mile before Houston stopped.

"Do you want to talk? First of all, I am Sam Houston and I just traded for you so that you may be returned to your family.""

"It would probably be better if I had been allowed to stay with the Caddo. After the initiation by the Indians, it wasn't a bad life. I know how people will look at me and the stories they will tell. I saw it happen to a woman in Kentucky when I was a little girl. She didn't live long after her return to her family."

"You will do all right because you are strong. Remember, talk can't hurt you, or I would be dead."

* * *

James talked Bill into helping him take Elizabeth home. Bill said for three dollars he could get a couple of men to come along. Bill wanted to return to Galveston and the two other men were heading in that direction anyway. Bill didn't feel bad about taking James' money after what he had heard about him.

He bought some supplies for the trip and Bill and the other two men were ready to leave. When Houston and Elizabeth rode up, he met them, he thanked Houston with his honey words and left before Houston could say anything. The group rode until dark and camped by a small stream.

He started his group out at daylight. After riding for an hour they heard a shot. Rounding the bend in the road, they came upon a cabin.

"Did you fire a shot?" James asked.

"I sure did. Two Indians were trying to steal my horses. Think I hit one of them."

"Let's take a look and see," James said as he dismounted and the group did likewise. They followed Smith into the brush looking for the dead Indian. They found the Indian, who was coming to. The shot had just grazed his forehead.

"That's the Indian who stripped and pinned Granny to the ground," Elizabeth said.

"Are you sure?" James asked, not taking his eyes off the Indian.

"Yes, he has cut scars on both of his arms. I was in his camp once and that is him. I will never forget him."

James shot him in the head, then turned and walked away. The group remounted and rode away. Bill and the other two men just looked at each other and grinned. The group rode for ten more days, when they come to a fork in the road. "Well, James, here is where we part company as this road leads to Galveston," Bill said, with the others nodding their heads.

He and Elizabeth took the right fork and Bill and the others took the left.

"Those men with Bill are a quiet bunch. I wonder if they can talk," he said.

"They can talk. I heard them whispering the night before last, but couldn't make out what they were saying."

"I will have you home tomorrow, Elizabeth. Martha will be so happy to see her sister again."

"Are you sure?"

"Yes, I made a promise to Martha that I wouldn't rest until all the captives were returned. You are the first. Do you know what happened to the rest?"

"The sixth day after the attack, I was taken by the Kiowa. Cynthia Ann, John, James, and Rachel were all taken by the Comanche."

Chapter 12

FOOT OF WICHITA MOUNTAINS.

OCTOBER 20, 1836.

Naduah was proud of herself; she spoke the Comanche tongue. She was always learning new words and never spoke in English. Arriving at the new campsite, she and Gray Foot put the tepee up without the help of Habbe.

Gray Foot told her many stories about the Old Ones: how the Old Ones moved from the cold country to the south searching for wild horses. Before they had horses, dogs were used to pull the travois loaded with supplies and tepee. The Old Ones were root eaters, but after getting horses, they turned from roots to meat. The killing of the buffalo became easier with the horse. Now, it was easier to raid and steal horses that were already broken to ride. She listened carefully to the stories that Gray Foot told her. She was beginning to understand the Comanche way of life.

She liked the new campsite because she could hear the flowing water of the river rippling over rocks. As she laid in her bed at night, she listened to the friendly sound of the water. She was happy cutting up the buffalo meat and preparing the buffalo hides. Peta was coming by every evening and they were going riding until sunset. He taught her how to control and handle Paint better. She was learning how to pick up objects off the ground while riding Paint at a dead run.

She spent much of the time daydreaming about riding Paint across the prairie in the fields of wild flowers. Peta was always in her dreams. She missed seeing and riding with him the most. He was like an older brother that she never had.

The next morning she woke up with cramps in her stomach. She still went about her morning work, thinking it was something she had eaten the night before. She went out and gathered wood for the fire, and returned loaded down with wood. As she stooped over, placing the wood on the ground, Gray Foot saw blood on her leg. "Naduah, you are no longer a girl; you are woman. Don't be afraid because now you are a women."

"What do you mean, now I am a woman?"

"You have passed from being a girl to becoming a young woman. The change will transform your whole life; you will see" Now, go inside the tepee and take off your clothes because I have other clothes for you to wear. I have been preparing for this day."

She wasn't sure what was happening, but Gray Foot's voice sounded excited. It must be good. She removed her buckskin dress when Gray Foot entered the tepee.

"First, you must wash the blood off, but don't wash your face. If you do, it will cause wrinkles before your time."

* * *

Gray Foot tied a piece of raw hide loosely around Naduah's waist; then in the back she hung a soft strip of deer skin. She walked around Naduah and pulled the skin between Naduah's legs. On the skin she placed soft dry moss to catch the excreta, pulling the surplus skin up and over the raw hide. Gray Foot handed her an old buckskin blouse that came to just above her knees.

"The blood will not hurt me because I am old and my medicine is weak, so I will stay here with you. You have to follow my advice. You cannot eat meat as it will make you sick at the stomach and cause you to flow more. You cannot comb or touch your hair because your hair will turn grey. Like I already told you, don't wash your face, and the moss we will burn in the fire inside the tepee. I will put a mark on the tepee so no one will enter. If Peta would touch anything that you have touched, he would lose his powerful medicine."

"How long will I be like this?"

"Not long, just four to six days, but it will come back regularly."

"My mother and her friends talked about the curse. Is this the curse?"

"I'm not sure what the word curse means, but to us, it's just burden."

Gray Foot knew that Peta would be coming to take Naduah for her evening ride. It had become a daily routine with him. She met him, "Can't you see the tepee is marked? This area is taboo to you," she said in a disgusted tone holding back a smile.

"No, I wasn't paying attention as I had other things on my mind."

62

"Warriors that have other things on their minds sometimes get themselves killed. You would be wise to remember it." Peta turned and left, while she watched him with a big smile on her face.

She cooked Naduah Indian potato with wild onions, since she couldn't eat meat. Her favorite dish was the bulbs of the sego lily cooked with crushed mesquite beans. The beans gave the bulbs a sweet taste because of their sugar content.

She washed the charcoal mark off the tepee on the fifth day. She had just finished when Iron Shirt came to the tepee. She had sent Naduah to the river to bathe herself as she must wash the taboo from her body.

"She is a woman now, but is she ready for marriage?" Iron Shirt asked, looking down.

"No, she is only beginning to learn The People's ways. She speaks the language, but she doesn't understand the full meaning of it yet."

"We need to speed up her training because Peta is very impatient."

"I thing we should make them work more together."

"That's a good idea. Peta is going on a buffalo hunt. He should take her to pack the meat and take care of the pack horses."

"I will tell her and have her ready to leave at sun-up."

"I will tell Peta. He will not be happy because he will have to show her how to pack the meat." They both laughed, and Iron shirt turned and walked away.

Before sunrise she awoke Naduah and gave her an old buckskin blouse with splits on both sides.

"Today, you are going on a buffalo hunt with Peta, so hurry and get Paint. You must do whatever Peta tells you because it can be dangerous, but he will watch out for you."

* * *

Peta came leading four pack horses. Each horse had a pack saddle like the one Gray Foot had used in moving the tepee. Naduah mounted Paint and he handed her the lead rope to the first horse. The other horses had their lead ropes braided in the horse's tail in front of him. He looked at her with a smile and said, "You stay close to me until I tell you different."

He led Naduah through the camp where many warriors and their women had met. When the leader of the hunt decided it was time to leave, he rode away followed by the rest. They rode over an hour before he stopped on a rise. He sat there for a while looking into a valley below. He whispered to Naduah, "You stay here with the other women and do what they do. When the hunt is over, you ride with the pack horse to me."

* * *

Naduah started to answer, but Peta and half the men rode to the left and the other half rode to the right. She, with the other women, sat quietly waiting and soon she heard animals running. The group moved up the ridge until they could see the warriors below. She saw that Peta and his group were attacking the buffalo from one direction while the other group came from the opposite.

She couldn't find Peta or Star because of the dust created by the buffalo. The buffalo started running in a circle with the warriors riding around the outer side.

She finally saw Peta riding along the left side of a buffalo. She saw him shoot an arrow into the side of the buffalo that turned toward Peta. Star swerved away from the buffalo, but wasn't quick enough to get clear. The buffalo hits Star sending Peta and Star to the ground. Star stumbled to his feet while Peta laid stretched out on the ground.

She was terrified that Peta was hurt and started to ride towards him. The woman closest to her grabbed Paint's rein and shook her head 'no'. It seemed to her that Peta had lain there motionless forever; then he moved. Star stood there looking down at him. Peta slowly stood up, mounted Star and rode after the herd.

She saw Peta was catching up with the herd when a cow broke out of the circle. Peta gave chase riding up from behind the cow. On the left side he shot an arrow in her. Star, at the same time, turned away and was clear of the cow. The leader of the hunt then called the hunt off because the buffalo needed to be killed quickly. The meat that was overheated from a long run would spoil before it could be dried.

* * *

Peta rode back to where he had killed the bull. Naduah looked at the woman who had stopped her before, and this time she nodded 'yes'. Naduah rode over the hill to where he had rolled the bull over on its side.

Naduah dismounted and asked, "Are you hurt? You took a bad fall with Star."

"No, I just had the wind knocked out of me. I'm all right now."

"You had me scared."

"Star tried to get away, but the bull was faster. My shot was off a little, so it was my fault also. It happens. Now, watch me load the pack horse."

He slit down the middle of the stomach and started skinning the hide off. After he had removed the hide from one side and back, he spread it out on the ground. He then cut the brisket across at the neck and folded it back. This allowed him to remove the forequarter at the joint which he carried and placed on a pack horse. He removed the hindquarter and placed it on the pack horse. He then rolled the buffalo over on the other side. He removed the other front and hindquarter. He sliced down the middle of the back, being careful not to cut the sinews which were removed intact. The sinews were used to make bow strings and thread. Then the flank was cut up towards the stomach and was removed with the brisket. He loaded ribs, entrails, horns, sinews, kidneys, liver, paunch, and hide. He left the heart because it was believed the heart held magical powers that prolonged the existence of the herd.

Naduah watched carefully how he packed the horses, because he had told her the next one was her job to pack. He finished butchering the bull. The only parts left were the heart, bare spine, and head. The tail had been skinned out with the hide.

He jumped on Star and rode to where the buffalo cow laid. Naduah followed leading the pack horses. The first thing he did was cut off the cows udder and drank the warm milk mixed with blood. This almost made Naduah sick.

"Here, you drink," as he pushed the udder in her face.

***

Naduah wasn't about to drink from the udder until she looked into his hard black eyes. She drank from fear and thirst. Shutting her eyes, she drank just a little. It tasted good, almost like cows milk for she couldn't taste the blood. She drank some more and Peta laughed.

She loaded the parts on the pack horse as Peta butchered the cow. She had trouble carrying the hindquarters. Peta carried them for her and just gave her a big grin. The buffalo cow was smaller than the bull and took less time to butcher and load. She saw that many of the other Indians were finished and heading back towards camp.

Gray Foot was standing in front of the tepee when they returned. Peta unloaded half of the cow's meat, the hide and the paunch. "That should keep you busy for a while," he said, giving her a big smile.

"If I only had my mother's knife to slice the meat, it would be a lot easier," she said. She picked up an old knife with the point broken off. Gray Foot had sharpened the knife for her on a sand rock.

* * *

Peta watched her slice the long thin strips of meat and hang them on the drying rack. Gray Foot was staking the hide, hair side down, in the sun to dry. He left thinking about what Naduah had said about needing a new knife.

He rode to the tepee of Muash and his squaw. Muash was now too old and crippled to hunt anymore. Their two sons and their families had died with the pox. Iron Shirt had taught him it was the warrior's responsibility to take care of the old without family. He gave the rest of the cow and the sinews to Muash. "You can use the sinew to make Naduah a new saddle. She needs a woman saddle, one that is deeper seated."

"I'm working on one that should fit her, but I'll need some hide to finish it."

"Will this bull's hide do?"

"Yes, I can tan half of it and make rawhide out of the rest."

"Then the hide is yours. Do you know anyone that has a good meat knife for trade?"

"Well, I do, cause Little Foot traded me a knife and some cloth that was taken on your Fort Parker raid for his new bow."

"What would you trade for the knife?"

"To you, nothing, because you are always bringing us meat. The others only want to trade me junk," Muash said as he went inside his tepee. He returned carrying the knife.

"That looks like a good meat knife. Are you sure I can't trade you something for it?" He stood looking at the knife. "It's sharp," he stated as he sucked the blood off his finger where he had cut himself.

"It should be. I spent a day sharpening it."

He left a part of the meat at his tepee for Sensa to dry and gave all the rest to Iron Shirt's four wives. After he unsaddled the horses, he turned them loose to graze. Walking back, he passed Gray Foot's tepee where he stood watching Naduah cutting the meat. Naduah stood with her back to him. Her arms and hands moved as if the wind was moving them in a smooth rhythm, and her golden hair moved in the breeze. Her graceful movements had him hypnotized. He didn't realize that Gray Foot was standing behind him until her voice broke the silence, "Peta, did you forget something?"

"No, I just came to give Naduah a new knife." His voice startled Naduah who turned to Peta with a smile.

"I traded for you a new knife. It's not your mother's knife, but it did come from Fort Parker," he said handing her the knife. Naduah looked it over carefully. It wasn't her mother's, but it was Granny's knife. She found Granny's mark on the handle. Naduah forget herself and gave him a big hug. She realized her mistake and stepped back quickly. "Thank you," she said, her face turning a beet red.

He wasn't use to that kind of emotion, dropped his eyes to the ground, turned, and walked away quickly. Gray Foot, with a twinkle in her eye, said very firmly, "You know that you are never to touch or show emotion towards warriors in public."

"I know, but I forgot. I was raised getting hugs from my mother, father, and my grandmother. I miss being hugged or someone hugging me more than missing my family."

"You can hug Peta anytime when the two of you are alone. It's all right then, but not in front of people."

Naduah went back to cutting the meat. Granny's knife was sharp, and because it was Granny's it had a personal meaning to her.

Chapter 13

James Parker was still looking for any news about the captives. One of the Coffee's Traders told him there were Indians camped on the Blue River near Captain Pace's place in Oklahoma. They were holding a white woman captive and the description sounded like his Rachel. He asked the Trader for directions to Pace's place. First, he had to cross the Red River.

He rode down to the Red River and found it flooded due to the heavy rain in the west. He was unable to cross on horseback and decided to build a raft. Walking down to the edge of the flood water, trying to decide where to build his raft, an elderly man approached him.

"She sure is a high one isn't she? I have lived here for a long time and I have never seen it this high."

"I need to cross. They tell me there is a tribe of Indians holding a white woman that sounds like my daughter."

"You must be that Parker fellow. I heard at the post you were around. My name is Stewart, but they call me 'Coon' cause mainly hunt raccoon for a living."

"I'm glad to meet you, Coon. Do you know where Captain Pace lives?"

"Not for sure because I have never been there, but from what I've heard it's about eighty miles straight north in Indian nation."

"I was thinking about building a raft to cross the Red."

"If I were you, I'd wait until the River went down. You know it's a far piece without a horse."

"I know, but if there is any chance that my daughter is with those Indians, I must go now. If I delay getting there anymore, they could leave for God only knows where."

"Well, if you're determined to cross the river, I will help you build a raft, but I still think you should wait."

"I can't wait, and I sure do accept your kind offer."

"Well, I'd better go and fetch an axe and some rawhide to tie the raft together so we can get started. While I'm gone you go down over yonder; there is a tree fall over there and you look around."

"I'll be there when you return." He turned and headed down along the river banks. He found the place where Coon meant; the trees, all sizes, were broken over and some of the bigger trees were uprooted. Together, they could easily get all the logs needed to make a raft. He started dragging some of the logs that were the right length for the raft. Finding a place where they could build next to water was the hardest part.

The flood water had raised up into the brushy area that ran along the river. He walked farther down the river and found an old road that hadn't been used in years. He could see where the wagon tracks were still visible, but in the center of the old road some small sprouts were growing. He went back to the tree fall and started pulling the smaller logs to the old road. He had enough logs to make his raft when Coon came back.

"I found an old road over there where we can build the raft close to water and not worry about getting caught in the thickets of the river bottoms,'" he said, pointing to where he had piled the logs.

"The road was the best crossing around here until it filled up with quicksand, so they moved it about two miles up river. This old river is bad about changing. The swift currents kept filling the holes with quicksand. When you come back, if you come back, be careful about where you cross," Coon said with a grin.

He and Coon set to work building the raft. They cut the small logs about all the same length placing them on other logs at the ends. They lashed the logs together with rawhide and finished the raft just before dark.

He returned to Coffee's Trading Post where the Kirkpatricks managed the Post. They asked him to spend the night with them. The next morning, he gave Kirkpatrick a letter to post if he hadn't returned in ten days. Mrs. Kirkpatrick gave him some bread and meat for his journey and he was on his way.

When he arrived at the raft Coon was waiting for him. Even though the raft was at the water's edge, it was difficult to move into the water. They had to cut small poles and use them as pries to inch the raft closer into the water. It was hot and the work was hard, but finally the raft was afloat. He shook Coon's hand and thanked him for his help and started poling his way across the bottoms.

When he hit the river's current, it swept his raft downstream. In his fight to get the raft across and through the brushy bottoms, he lost his food and other supplies. The raft became lodged in brush and he had to wade through the bottoms in water above his waist. The tall grass in the bottom and high water forced him to struggle just to move forward. He was exhausted by the time he reached the prairie.

It was almost sundown and the prairie grass was two feet high so walking was slow and difficult. He set his course of direction with his pocket compass in a northerly direction. He was tired and laid down on a bed of grass and fell asleep.

He awoke around midnight to flashes of lightning and thunder. The driving rain came as if poured from the dark sky. The lightning stopped and it was impossible for him to know which direction to go because he couldn't see his compass. The flat prairie was filling up with water, and was now over a foot deep. The wind changed direction blowing hard cold rain mixed with snow. His clothes were starting to crack when he moved; they were freezing upon him.

He made a large circle mashing down the grass which by now was held together by the freezing snow and ice. He kept himself walking around the circle until daylight, then returned to his directed course. His hands and feet were hurting from the cold, but he trudged forward with every step being harder to take. He saw a woods to his right and moved in that direction.

Hours later, staggering and stumbling, he came to the wooded area. Unable to move any farther, he sat down on an old log to rest, but being tired and cold, he became sleepy so he dozed. Waking, he knew if he didn't move he would freeze to death. What he needed was a fire to warm his hands, feet, and dry his clothes. Trying to stand up, he realized that he couldn't, but after working himself around, he was able to pull himself with one hand and push himself up with the other.

He saw an old rotten log lying on the ground and moved painfully towards it. After tearing away wet wood, he found dry rotten wood with his cold suffering hands. He cut small pieces of cotton from his shirt. He removed his pistol that was wrapped in his shirt which he carried under his arm. He loaded the pistol with powder, rammed the pieces of cotton in the barrel, and held the barrel close to the dry wood and discharged it. The cotton caught on fire and started a fire in the dry wood. He warmed his hands and feet over the fire. They went from being almost paralyzed and started to hurt. After he warmed himself, he laid down on the wet ground and went to sleep. When he awoke his clothes were frozen to the ground. He was able to rebuild the fire and warmed himself before he started on his journey to Pace's.

For the next two days he traveled both night and day, only stopping to rest and taking short naps. He wasn't sure if he had passed Pace's place, or if it was still farther. Not wanting to spend another night in this wilderness, he pushed forward. It was then that he heard a calf bawl. He knew if there was cattle around there had to be a Settlement near by. This made him forget how hungry and tired his body was, and he hurried toward the sound of the calf.

He saw an outline of a cabin in the dark and a light in the window. He knocked on the door. A large pleasant looking lady comes to the door and he said, "I'm James Parker and I'm looking for Captain Pace.'"

"He isn't here right now, but can I help you?"

"I have traveled for four days. I'm from Texas where I was told there were Indians close by with a white captive. I came to see if she is my daughter."

"The Captain should be back any minute. Come on in and sit by the fire and have a cup of coffee."

He went inside the cabin, sat by the fire, and drank the coffee. He drank it in two large gulps; the hot liquid filled his empty stomach. Mrs. Pace noticing this asked, "Have you eaten anything today?" while refilling his coffee cup.

"No, Ma'am, not since day before yesterday."

"Well, you just move over there to the table and I will get you something to eat."

Mrs. Pace sliced some meat and fresh baked bread. His stomach felt like it had died and gone to heaven. He ate slowly because he had gone a long time on very little food. It didn't take much to fill him up. He had just finished eating when Captain Pace entered with a surprised look on his face. However, his wife quickly explained the situation.

"I'm sorry, Mr. Parker. The Indians did bring in a woman captive, but she was Mrs. Yorkins," replied Captain Pace.

The Paces invited him to stay there that night and Mrs. Pace fed him a big breakfast. After he had eaten his fill, he left the Pace's cabin and found some of Coffee's traders. He asked them about news of his daughter, Rachel; only one knew anything about her.

"Mr. Parker, I was in a Comanche's Camp up on the Arkansas and I think a story I heard was about your daughter."

"What did you hear?"

"Seems a band of the Yamparikas Comanche have this woman captive who was pregnant, a captive from Fort Parker."

"Yes, yes, that would be my daughter. Tell me about her!"

"This captive is a slave and they work her hard, the way I get the story. She has a baby boy that is small and cried a lot. She was paying more attention to the baby than her work. The old man who owned her paid a warrior two buffalo hides to kill the child."

"My God, my God, this can't be true?"

"All that I know is that 'He That Walks Crooked' told me the story, and in the past he has never lied to me."

He went numb all over. He didn't know what to say or do. Turning, with his head down, he made his way back to the Pace's cabin. He was sad from the news that his grandchild had been killed, but rejoicing that Rachel was still alive. Telling Mrs. Pace that he was leaving, she fixed him some meat and bread for his journey. He set his course straight south towards the Red River.

He arrived on the Red River which was still very high and built a fire. Dragging up logs, he burned them to get the right length for the raft. He then tied the logs together with grape vines and finished the raft at sundown. He laid down and went to sleep. It had been twenty days since he first crossed the Red. His family should be receiving the letter he had left with Mr. Kirkpatrick to mail and would assume by his message he was dead.

The next morning he crossed the Red. It was easier than the first time, but he ended up farther down stream. The water was lower in the bottoms which hung the raft up in the brush. He waded in water just above his knees until he reached an incline. He hurried to the Trading Post.

"Parker, you're alive! We thought something happened to you because you've been gone so long," Kirkpatrick said.

"Did you send my letter?"

"No, there hasn't been anyone headed in that direction."

"I'm glad, 'cause you can see I'm still alive," he said with a little smile.

He stayed with the Kirkpatricks, resting and filling up on Mrs. Kirkpatrick's food. He was sitting outside the post in the shade when Kirkpatrick came out.

72

"What are your plans now?" Kirkpatick asked.

'I'm not sure, but when I left home Congress was in session at Columbia. I think maybe I should go down there and ask them for a company of Rangers."

"From what I hear, our new President Houston is for making a treaty with Indians instead of walloping them," Kirkpatrick said.

"Well, I'm hoping that Congress looks at it different. I know our new Secretary of State, Stephen Austin, is more in favor of putting the Indians in their place," he said as he mounted his horse.

Arriving in Columbia, he found Congress had adjourned. He went and talked to General Rusk and Major Burton; both agreed that the Indians should be taught a lesson for taking white captives. However, they were helpless to help him in any way. The only way they could help was with an order from Houston and Sam was sticking by his guns. Houston believed a treaty was the only way the young Republic could live with the Indians. He, disappointed, returned to his home with the only good news for Martha--Rachel was still alive.

Chapter 14

Naduah stormed around the fire and tepee like a mad bull. Gray Foot laughed to herself and said, "Peta will be back, you'll see. You had better get used to him being gone on raids. This was the first raid since the raid on Fort Parker."

"Who is leading the raid, and who are they raiding this time?"

"High Wolf is leading the raid into Mexico to steal horses and take captives. The Mexicans have many good horses and they are easily stolen."

"What if something happens to him?"

"My dear child, if the Great Spirit wanted Peta, he would take him no matter where he is. Just because he is in Mexico doesn't make his chances any greater. His horse may even step into a hole while hunting buffalo and kill him. But remember, he has the medicine of the Eagle to watch over him."

"There is still no one to ride with me, now that he's gone," she replied, not wanting Gray Foot to think she missed his company. But she did miss his company. He had been gone now over a week. Peta came by every day to talk or they would go riding; time passed so slowly without him. She was missing him more than she did her own family.

"I will find someone to ride with you if it will change your mood," Gray Foot answered taking a deep breath.

"I don't want to ride with someone else. I want to ride with Peta."

"Well, maybe you should have gone to Mexico with him," Gray Foot said, turning away, because she couldn't hold back her laughter.

"I would have, but he didn't ask me," she murmured softly."

* * *

74

Gray Foot slipped away from the tepee while Naduah was picking up fire wood. Iron Shirt was sitting in front of his tepee. It was a rare occasion when he was by himself. "My son, we have a problem. Naduah misses Peta. She says that it's because their is no one to ride with her. You know that they went riding everyday."

"I will send someone to ride with her, but it will not be a brave."

"Thank you, my son," hurrying back to the tepee before Naduah returned.

* * *

The next day as Naduah was returning from the spring, she saw Iron Shirt talking to Gray Foot, and with them stood a tall warrior.

"Naduah, this is Eagle Woman who will ride with you and teach you many things that Peta can't."

She looked hard at Eagle Woman because she looked like a man. She wore clothes like a warrior and her hair was cut like a warrior; there was nothing about her that looked like a woman.

Iron Shirt saw the expression on her face, "Believe me, she is a woman; but she can fight like and better than a man. She has proven it on many occasions. You should listen to her and you will learn. She will teach you things that some day will help keep you and your family stay alive."

She couldn't believe her eyes as she stared at Eagle Woman. She couldn't ever remember seeing her in camp before. Since she looked more like a warrior, she wouldn't have given her a glance. Eagle Woman was tall, flat-chested, bow-legged, and slim-hipped with shoulders larger than the rest of her body. The expression on her face was blank, with piercing eyes.

"Naduah, I will be back at sunrise," she said and turned walking quickly away.

She was afraid of this strange woman. She stood there watching Eagle Woman's graceful movements as she seemed to disappear into the camp. She wasn't looking forward to riding with Eagle Woman because she wanted to be riding with Peta. Oh, when was he coming back?

The next morning at daylight Eagle Woman just seemed to appear from nowhere. Eagle Woman turned away and, without saying a word, started walking towards the path that led to where the horses were grazing. She quietly followed her and caught Paint. As she looked around, there sat Eagle Woman on her horse. She mounted Paint and started riding towards her. Eagle Woman turned her horse putting him in a dead run away from her. Paint couldn't catch up; finally, she pulled him to a walk. If this was the way Eagle Woman wanted to ride, she could ride by herself.

She waited until Eagle Woman had passed over a ridge out of sight and turned Paint towards a cottonwood area. She rode him as hard as she could, passing through the woods, turning Paint into an arroyo, then slowing him down and riding him into the small creek. The rocky bottom would leave no tracks. She saw a dry gulch ahead that led to the pasture where the horses were.

She rode Paint into the middle of the herd, dismounted, took his bridle off, and moved quickly through the herd. She entered the cottonwood grove into a dense thicket where she could watch her back trail. She had just seated herself when out of the dry gulch came Eagle Woman. She was riding slowly following Paint's tracks. Eagle Woman stopped and started looking over the herd for Paint. Paint was easily spotted because he was the only horse in the herd that was wet with sweat. Eagle Woman rode around the horse herd looking for Naduah's tracks.

She sat there almost holding her breath, but she was well-hidden. If she had left a track, Eagle Woman was sure to find it. Eagle Woman rode on past her. She waited and slowly made her way through the thicket and out the other side. She saw Gray Foot removing the dry meat from the meat rack on the other side of the tepee. She edged her way along the opposite side of the tepee and slipped inside. She sat at the side of the door where no one could see her from the outside.

"Have you seen Naduah?" Eagle Woman asked, grinding out the words between clenched teeth.

"Why, no, she left with you. Did you lose her, or just misplace her? You had better go and tell Iron Shirt."

The camp crier was running through the camp calling out that High Wolf's raiding party had returned from Mexico. She ran out of the tepee and asked, "When will they be here?"

"They will ride in as soon as the people have gathered and are ready to receive them." Gray Foot said, turning to Eagle Woman, "I guess that Naduah wasn't misplaced after all."

"I am glad, I would have hated to explain to Iron Shirt what happened," her eyes narrowing with contempt as she looked at Naduah.

She was glad to see her leave because she had all these questions for Gray Foot.

"Will Peta be with them?"

"Yes, since the crier announced their return, means no one was killed; yet, there could be wounded. We will just have to wait and see. We must quickly change our clothes and hurry and join the women singers."

She and Gray Foot hurried across the camp to where the warriors were in a line, then the women formed up inside the men's lines. As the raiding party came into view, the warriors started dancing and yelling, and the women started singing and walking toward the raiding party. When the raiding party passed, the women fell in behind them singing.

She saw Little Foot riding Star and holding Peta who was wounded. She started to run for Peta, but Gray Foot grabbed her and held her back keeping her with the singers as they moved behind the raiding party. She was no longer singing as she kept trying to see Peta. Iron Shirt saw what was happening as he was at the head of the warrior line.

She never took her eyes off Peta; she saw Iron Shirt say something to Little Foot. The braves of the raiding party all went straight to their tepee. Gray Foot was pulling her along, but she was trying to find Peta. She had lost sight of him after the parade entered the tepee area. "Come on, we must hurry home. We have work to do now."

"What about Peta? He is hurt," she sobbed.

"You will see him soon; now come along."

Gray Foot hurried her along, and when they arrived at Gray Foot's tepee, Little Foot was coming out. 'I laid him down. He was tired from the trip home. The bullet went through his left shoulder and came out the back side. He was very lucky. A little higher and it would have hit a bone."

'Thanks, Little Foot, we will take care of him,' Gray Foot said as she hurried into the tepee with Naduah right behind her. Gray Foot felt Peta's head, and said, "Naduah, go to the spring and bring back some cold water."

"I want to stay with him."

"I said, go. You'll be sick of him before this is over. Now, go!"

She headed for the spring, and ran most of the way. She filled the buffalo paunch full of cold water; it was almost more than she could carry. Gray Foot handed her a buffalo horn filled with water. Gray Foot then placed a rolled up buffalo hide behind him, so he was sitting up and could drink.

"He is burning up and needs to drink a lot of water. I must go and dig some roots for medicine, but when the Medicine Man comes, you will have to stay outside, or you will ruin his medicine." Gray Foot was gone before she could reply.

* * *

Iron Shirt came with the Medicine Man who carried three bags and two Eagle feathers. The Medicine Man went inside and started chanting and singing his song calling on his medicine. He knelt down and passed the Eagle feathers over Peta three or four times. He opened one of his bags, took out some ground herbs, and placed them in Peta's mouth. He opened the second bag taking out rocks that were different in color. He held them one at a time passing over Peta's body. He opened the third bag, took out a head of an owl, and waved it over Peta. All this time he was reciting a spell to produce big medicine to cure Peta.

Iron Shirt and Naduah stood outside of the tepee and watched. As soon as the Medicine Man finished, he came outside. She noticed he was wet with sweat and seemed tired. He staggered when he walked. Iron Shirt and the Medicine Man walked away and she entered the tepee and gave Peta a drink of water. It was the first time he looked her in the eyes and gave her a small smile. She knew the Medicine Man's medicine had been strong because that was the first time he had smiled.

* * *

Gray Foot returned with the herbs she had been hunting. The roots she placed in an old kettle of water and set on the fire. After the roots had boiled she added leaves to the boiling water. She removed the kettle from the fire and dipped some of the herbal tea into a wooden bowl and set it aside. She scooped the leaves out of the water and placed them on a small piece of flint hide.

She carried the bowl and the hide inside to where Peta sat, and with a clean rag she washed his wounds. Then, taking the leaves, she pressed them on his shoulder around the wound. The leaves stuck to his skin. She continued until his shoulder was covered front and back with the leaf poultice. She dipped a little of the herbal tea out of the kettle. She filled the buffalo horn with water, adding a few drops of the herbal tea, and handed it to Naduah. "You make sure that he drinks this before you give him anymore water."

* * *

Naduah sat at Peta's side looking at him and giving him the herbal tea. As their eyes met, Peta would give her a little smile, but she could tell he was in great pain most of the time. He said nothing; his eyes were fixed on the tepee wall. She wished he would say something, if only her name. Gray Foot entered carrying a small horn spoon and a wooden bowl. "If you can get him to eat this, I powdered some dry meat and added water so it should make him stronger as he has lost a lot of blood."

"Will he be all right? He looks bad, even in the eyes."

"He will live. You just wait and see, but now you take good care of him."

"I will, you know I will," she said reaching down and holding Peta's hand. Gray Foot grinned and left the tepee; the best medicine he could get was Naduah. She would give him the will to live more than anything else.

The next day Peta was better because his eyes weren't fixed in a stare, and now and then he would smile at her. She now was mixing the herbal tea into his water and feeding him. Gray Foot stayed outside the tepee, but very little that went on inside missed her. Naduah wasn't sure if it was the Medicine Man's medicine, or the herbal tea and poultice of Gray Foot that was making him better. Iron Shirt came by every day to see how Peta was doing.

A week later Peta was well enough to stand, but it took him a while, with Naduah's help, for him to stand alone. After standing a while, he laid down and went to sleep. She kept checking him to see if he was awake. Gray Foot was losing her patience with Naduah. She would start tanning a hide, work a while, then go to see if Peta was wake. She was so deep in thought, she would forget what she was doing. Gray Foot never said a word to Naduah, but just laughed to herself. She remembered when she was young and how different things were.

Everyday he stood up longer and started to walk around the tepee, both inside and out. Little Foot came to talk to Peta, and they talked a long time in the tepee. When Little Foot was ready to leave, Peta left with him. Naduah didn't like it, but there was nothing she could do about it but sulk. Because now that he was well, he would go back to his own tepee. Peta came back by himself and the poultice had dried out in the sun and fallen off.

* * *

Gray Foot wasn't happy with him and told him. "Now, see what you have done. I will have to make a new poultice. I have more important work to do than work on you." Gray Foot handed Naduah a bowl which had the herbal tea in it. "Wash his shoulder good and hard."

Peta sat down in front of the tepee and Naduah started washing his wound. When she moved to the back of his shoulder where the bullet had come out, he yelled with pain.

"See, you aren't healed yet." Gray Foot announced angrily, more for Naduah's benefit than Peta's.

She put the leaf poultice back on his shoulder, but this time she covered it and tied his arm up. She didn't tell him that most of the infection was gone and had started to heal. She wanted to keep him with Naduah as long as she could. She and Iron Shirt had a long talk whenever he came to visit. They would walk away from the tepee and talk very quietly to each other.

Weeks had passed before she let Peta move back into his own tepee with Sensa. Naduah was happy because they rode every day.

Chapter 15

MONROE, TEXAS.

MARCH 2, 1837

James Parker decided that Sam Houston wouldn't give him permission to raise a company to go after the Indians. He had learned from his last trip that the Indians were holding Rachel some place on the Arkansas River. His new plan was to get all the traders on the Red River to trade for Rachel, John Platt, John, and Cynthia Ann.

He needed money to give the traders in advance to pay for the hostages' return. He passed through the little Settlement of Monroe following the road that led straight to the Red River. The road was surrounded by tall pine trees that reached the blue sky above. He found the long leaf pine tree he was looking for. The pine tree had been burned when it was young. He rode on past the tree, riding into the pines on the west side, and tied his horse. Circling back to the road, he sat down where he could watch the road in both directions.

When he was sure there wasn't anybody in sight, he slipped across the road into the woods of pines not following a trail. The rays of light shining down through the trees guided his direction straight east. He picked his way carefully through the pine trees until he arrived at a cabin by a small clear stream.

He stopped and yelled, "Moses, it's me, James Parker." He saw the old rifle withdraw from a slot in the logs of the cabin. The cabin door opened and out stepped a big framed man with a long red beard.

"I heard you coming. The way you walk on those pine cones, they could hear you for miles."

"You sure are in a good humor today."

"Come on inside and quiet down," Moses answered.

James said no more and went inside the cabin. Inside he asked, "Do we have a problem?"

"I'm not sure. There have been two fellows moving around in the woods for a week, but they don't come to the cabin. They just watch me from a distance."

"Before I left, I went to Galveston and picked up some more paper," James said as he opened his saddlebag and pulled out a package wrapped in oil cloth.

"This is the last time you need to pick up paper for me."

"Why! Are you quitting?"

"No, I'm moving to Galveston Island. I don't like them watching me."

"I need three thousand, if you have that much made up?" James said.

"What are you going to do with that much money?"

"I'm going to deposit it with three different traders, so they can buy goods to trade for Parker captives."

"Don't you think you're taking a big chance putting that many counterfeit banknotes together in one place?" Moses asked.

"Not the way I have it planned. I will count the bills out in thousand dollar piles, put them in an oil cloth and place my seal on the package. I am going to give a package to the trader along the Red River. They aren't to open the package until they trade for a Parker captive."

"I have fives and tens, all on the Bank of Illinois at Shawneetown. I have made them all look old, but be careful.

"It's a long way back to Illinois. The notes will pass through many hands before reaching there," James said.

"I'm going to quit for a while and let it cool down around here. Whoever is watching me is after something; so when you leave out the front, I'm going out the back."

"Where are you going to be on the island?"

"I don't know for sure yet, but somewhere near the west end. It is less populated there."

"I will find you," James said as he opened the front door and disappeared into the woods. He moved quietly through the woods, stopping every now and then to listen if someone was following. It was hard to walk through the pine trees without stepping on pine cones. He stepped into the middle of a new growth of pines and was well-hidden; he could hardly see out.

He heard movement coming towards him, keeping his eyes on the direction where he heard the last movement. The only sound he heard was his own breathing and it grew louder. Whoever was following him had stopped, also. They must not have known where he left his horse, or they would be waiting for him there.

He stood listening to the pine warblers that were singing in the bigger pine trees to his right. Whoever was following hadn't moved any closer because the pine warblers kept singing their song. He still hadn't heard any movement out in the pines. Then, like a crash, the woods was alive; he heard the sound of something coming fast in his direction. There was more than one sound. Then right in front of him four deer passed on a dead run. Whoever was following him had scared the deer. He took off running as fast as his legs would carry him right behind the deer. The deer led him to the road and they crossed and kept on going. He wasn't far from his horse, which he quickly mounted, and then headed north towards the Red River. He rode for two hours before he came to the Sabine River. The water was low in the river so he turned west into the river and rode until sundown. He came upon an old game trail that led north and decided to follow it.

His horse was tired, so he dismounted and led him. The moon was bright and the trail was easy to follow. He rode and walked his horse until well after midnight and moved off into the woods where he found a grassy spot for his horse to graze.

Picketing his horse he laid down close by to rest. Sleeping lightly, he awakened when his horse snorted. He saw his ears were pointed in the direction of the river. He ran straight to his horse, holding the horse by the nose and rubbing him, so he wouldn't neigh to the other horses.

He wasn't sure if the riders were the ones following him, but not taking any chances, he waited until they were out of hearing distance. He was headed for Jonesboro on the Red River, but decided now to go straight to the Coffee Trading Post at Pottsboro. He knew it would take him a while to make his way across country because he didn't know any trails that led there.

He rode out of the pine trees and into a woodland of post oak trees. He followed the game trails that ran in a northwesterly direction. The limbs of the trees drooped so low to the ground that he had to walk and lead his horse. He walked out of the wooded area onto the prairie. The waving grass in the wind was like a breath of fresh air. He had spent two days slowly moving through the woods.

He decided to ride straight north on the prairie; he could see the outline of the timber to his left. He wasn't sure where he was, or how far it was to the Red River. He knew he wasn't going to head into the timber again as it was just too slow going.

He arrived on the Red River two days later but wasn't sure where he was. The men who had followed him were east of where he was, so the west would be the best direction for him to take. He hadn't traveled far when the Red River Road that ran straight west left the Red River. He decided to follow the road west as he saw there were many tracks of horses going in the same direction.

He followed the road on the second day and arrived at Pottsboro. In Pottsboro, Holland Coffee was rebuilding the trading post. Luck was holding for James as Holland Coffee was there himself bossing the construction of the new enlarged trading post.

"Mr. Coffee, I would like to make a deal with you. I have with me $1000 in bank notes which I wrapped in oil cloth and placed my seal on the bag, if you would be so kind to accept it. The money is to be used anytime to buy supplies to trade to the Indians for a Parker captive."

"I will gladly be of service to you and your family, but you don't have to put up the money 'till I make the trade."

"Yes, but what if something happens to me? This way you can go ahead and make the trade because you have the money. You do know that I expect you to keep the package sealed until you have need for it."

"Yes, I will not use your money until there is need to make a trade."

He felt that Coffee's word was good and agreed to his terms. He turned and walked back to his horse and removed the oil cloth bag. Handing the bag to Coffee, he said, "I hope that you have to open it soon."

"So do I Mr. Parker, so do I."

He walked back to his horse and rode away. He still had the Marshall Trading Post and the Smith Trading Post to visit. He wasn't going to make a deal with Colwell & Wallace. For some reason he didn't trust Wallace. He was too much like himself. James felt good and was smiling inside as he rode east, because he always felt good when he had cheated someone.

He made the same deal with Marshall and Smith and headed home. His horse was getting pretty well worn out, but that had never been a problem before. He would just have to steal one.

He saw smoke rising to his right and rode in that direction. Riding towards the smoke, he came upon a clearing. At the edge of the clearing was a small cabin that sat by a small stream of running water. Behind the cabin was a small corral with three horses running loose, but one horse was tied outside.

He moved around in the woods until he could ride right up behind the cabin, blocking the view of the person clearing the land. The horse was saddled and ready to go. He quickly changed the saddle from one horse to the other, mounted, and rode the horse away back into the woods the same way he had entered.

He arrived home two days later. The horse he had stolen was a good one and he would like to keep him, but he knew better and turned him loose.

Chapter 16

Gray Foot and Naduah had been on the move now for four days. They just topped the last summit. Looking down into the valley of the Arkansas River, they couldn't believe their eyes. As far as they could see there were tepee lined up on both sides of the river. The tepee sat almost against each other, together as closely as possible.

"I have never seem so many tepee together in one place," she said.

"Why are they all here?"

"Iron Shirt's band and tribes of all the Plains Indians are meeting together for the first time. Tribes, who are bitter enemies, are now meeting in peace. This has all been made possible by Manual Flores' plan to drive the new white settlers out. The Mexican government is hoping to set up a buffer zone between the United States and Texas with the Indians," she replied.

"We will never get a camp site close to the river," Naduah said, looking up and down the river. She saw Peta and High Wolf riding toward Iron Shirt who was now on the floor of the valley.

"It looks like they found us a campsite," Gray Foot said.

"We can't be close to the river. From here it looks as if we are miles away," Naduah replied pointing in both directions.

Grey said with a little grin, "High Wolf will pick the best site available for us. Don't you worry."

They watched as Iron Shirt started the group moving again led by Peta and High Wolf. They turned in a westerly direction and traveled over a mile before they crossed the Arkansas River. There they found many of the other Comanche tribes all camped together.

"See, we aren't far from the river."

"We are closer than I figured we would be," Naduah said.

They started putting up their tepee and unpacking, and settled into their new campsite before dark.

* * *

Naduah was surprised when she saw Peta walking towards them. She hadn't seen Peta for over five days and she had missed him more than she realized, until she saw him. He stopped and talked to Gray Foot, not even looking in her direction. She felt a little hurt. She wasn't going to move towards him. If he wanted to talk to her, he would have to come to where she was staking down the tepee. Her heart skipped a beat as she moved behind the tepee.

* * *

Peta saw Naduah going around the tepee. Now, he would have to walk around behind just to see her. Gray Foot would know the reason he had come. A little embarrassed, he kept rubbing the ground with his right foot and looking at the tepee, hoping that she would come on around the other side.

He watched her as she came back around the tepee and drove the last stake into the ground. He looked at her and smiled, "If I'm not busy tomorrow, we can go riding. There is a lot of new country around here."

"Well, if I'm not busy, I may just go with you," Naduah replied. As soon as she said it, she was sorry, but couldn't take it back. She was having her second period and didn't realize why she felt so miserable.

He turned away. Boy, was she in a good mood today, he thought as he made his way through the campground. He was getting use to Naduah's moods. She wasn't the pleasant little girl now like she was when he first captured her.

* * *

Gray Foot hadn't missed a thing. She had seen the look on Naduah's face when Peta came. It made her remember back when she was Naduah's age; there were many times her feelings had been hurt by the one she loved.

* * *

John Parker was also there with the Chief Wild Horse band and it was the first time he had seen James Platt Plummer since they were both captured when the Indians attack Fort Parker. He couldn't believe he had changed so much in such a short time, but he still knew it was him. As he ran towards him, James Platt ran away. He looked around all the tepee and finally gave up.

* * *

James Platt Plummer ran into Chief Shaking Hand's tepee and watched John Parker go by. Nooki, his Indian mother, looked at him and smiled. Toniet was always running into the tepee and hiding from the bigger boys. Toniet wasn't sure why he ran away from him because he looked like John Parker. But, with his dark dirty skin, he looked just like another Indian, and the Indian boys that size were always chasing him.

He worked his way out of the tepee watching John weave his way through the other tepee. He followed John through the village keeping at a safe distance and ducking behind a tepee whenever John stopped and looked back. As he ran from John, he didn't realize that he ran within eight feet of his mother.

* * *

Rachel was on her way to where the Chief's Council was meeting. By now Rachel had learned the Comanche language, and knew it was against the Comanche's law for women to listen in on the council meetings. She was wearing an old ragged buckskin dress covered with dirt and grease from cleaning buffalo hides.

* * *

The camp was too crowded for Naduah, so she returned quickly back to Gray Foot's tepee. She hoped that she hadn't made Peta mad and that he would still take her riding tomorrow like he had promised. It was getting harder to hold down her feelings for him. She was always saying the wrong things to him when he was around and then felt sorry after she had said them.

The next day Peta came at noon, and he brought Paint with him. She raced to meet Paint, talking and rubbing his coat, and acting like Peta wasn't even there. Peta stood and watched her as he talked to Gray Foot. Finally, Peta mounted Star. Seeing this, she sprang on Paint and they rode away, leaving Gray Foot smiling to herself because they were made for each other.

She and Peta rode toward the summit. They stopped and looked at all the tepee that lined the river. "Have you ever seen so many tepee in one place?" she asked.

"No, this is the first time, so my father said, that all the Plains Indians have met together."

"What is the meeting for?"

"If all the tribes can agree, they will organize one big effort to drive the Whites out of our country."

"I didn't know there were this many Comanche in the whole world"

"There aren't only the Comanche here, but the Sioux, the Pawnee, the Crow, the Caddo, and the Kiowa."

"How long will we be here?"

"We stay here until all the tribal Chiefs agree in council when and how we are to run the Whites out."

Without realizing it, Peta and she started walking down the summit away from the camp. She was ahead of Peta. He couldn't keep his eyes off her. Her hair shone in the glowing sun. Her pale skin was a dark brown. She looked so beautiful. How much longer must he wait before she was his? They walked in silence, each with their own thoughts.

She jumped on Paint's back and yelled, "I can beat you to the trees." Paint was running hard before Peta knew what was happening. He mounted Star and pushed as fast as the pony could run. Peta had somewhat closed the gap between them, but the distance was too great.

She beat him and jumped to the ground laughing. Peta didn't like to be beaten at anything, and to have her beat him and laugh at him made him even madder. He jumped off Star and ran straight for her. He grabbed her and started to shake her. Then he looked into those beautiful blue eyes. She looked at him with a big smile with no sign of fear and kissed him.

This wasn't the first time she had ever kissed him, and his whole body felt warm and different. Peta pulled back and looked at her. It was the first time he saw her as a young woman. Peta was now quietly moving away leading Star. She couldn't figure out why Peta changed so quickly, for it was like he was in a different world. Was it because she had kissed him? She grabbed Paint and followed him.

She had always kissed the people she loved. She felt like she had done something wrong, but Peta was living on the white clouds that were floating below the bright blue sky. They walked in silence.

* * *

Peta felt he would have to tell Iron Shirt about what had happened. Maybe it was time for him to claim Naduah for his wife. They rode into camp, and neither of them spoke a word. Gray Foot knew something was wrong by just looking at them, but said nothing. He didn't dismount from Star, but grabbed Paint's reins and she slid off Paint. He led Paint away and she ran into the tepee where she started crying.

* * *

Gray Foot smiled to herself and thought of the lovers' first fight. She busied herself for a while until she figured Naduah had enough time to bring herself under control. Entering the tepee Gray Foot said, "Tell me what happened."

"I kissed him and it made him mad at me."

She laughed, "You didn't make him mad. He just realized that you are grown up, that's all. He has been treating you as his little sister, but from now on he will be treating you as his lover."

"I like it the way it was," Naduah said.

"It's time; you are old enough for it to happen."

She wasn't going to say anymore about it because they would be breaking camp in a few days. The courtship between the two would have to wait until they returned to a more permanent campsite.

* * *

Rachel Plummer had attended the council meeting every day even though women weren't suppose to hear what went on in council. She was beaten and driven away. She would circle the council meeting, then work her way back to where she could hear. The council was in agreement that they could all join together and drive the Whites out of the area. What they couldn't agree on was when they were going to do it. Some tribes wanted it to start in two years while others wanted to start in three years. The council broke up leaving the decision to the Northern Indians, who would send messages to Southern Indians when they felt the time was right.

She had moved through the camp every day, but hadn't seen any of the other captives. John and her son, James Platt, were all over the camp every day. Naduah was camped farther away. The council meetings ended after seven days and the tribes started moving out three days later. The tribes all took part in the three days of ceremony. Each tribe held a dance. This showed that they believed in the council's decision and would participate when the time came. Iron Shirt's band was among the first to leave. They packed up and headed for Texas.

* * *

Chief Shaking Hands renamed James, Toniets, which meant Runs Fast, because he could out run all the other boys his size. Since Toniets' capture at Fort Parker, he had learned to adapt to the Comanche ways. He learned that crying didn't help him get what he wanted on the long ride from Fort Parker, and now he felt comfortable riding a horse.

Chapter 17

MONTGOMERY COUNTY, TEXAS.

JUNE 19, 1837

James Parker was still thinking about the captives: his daughter, Rachel, and her son, James Platt, and his brother's children, Cynthia Ann and John. The attack on Fort Parker had happened over one year ago; the only captive released was Elizabeth Kellogg.

He decided he would find Sam Houston and ask him again for a company of Rangers. He had heard that Houston's Treaty with the Indians had failed and he was ready to send a company of Rangers. He hurried to the new city of Houston and met with Sam Houston, who finally agreed to give him the right to raise a company. James would be the Commander-in-Chief of the company called "Independent Volunteers of Texas." He could enlist as many men as were willing to join him on the expedition into Indian country.

He had written letters to his two brothers, Nathaniel and Joseph, asking them to come to help him find the captives. He was expecting Joseph any day. Nathaniel would be longer getting there because he still lived in Illinois. He wasn't going to wait for them to arrive. He started enlisting members into the company in Houston. The volunteers with families, who agreed to join the company, returned to their homes to set their affairs in order. They spread the word that he was organizing a company and when they returned, brought many volunteers back.

When he and his group entered a community, it wasn't long before a group had gathered. He was like his father, Elder John, and his brother, Daniel, who could work a crowd into a frenzy. He was careful how he outlined his plan, but led them to believe if the Indians didn't turn over the captives, he would make them wish they had.

He made his way north to Nacogdoches when Joseph finally caught up with him. Joseph had heard on the road that he was raising a company of men. He had collected over a 100 men by now with more joining every day. He was on his way to the Jonesboro Crossing on the Red River when his brother, Nathaniel, caught up with the group. They camped on the Texas side of the Red River waiting for all his volunteers to catch up.

That night he outlined his plans to his brothers. He would lead the company through the Indian Territory asking the Indians about the captives. He was sure as they worked their way west an Indian somewhere would know the location of a tribe that was holding captives.

He was up at sunrise. The group was ready to cross the Red River when a rider came riding hard into camp.

"I'm looking for James Parker."

"That's him right over there."

"James Parker, I have a dispatch for you from Sam Houston," the rider said handing him the letter.

He opened the letter, started reading, and a look of disgust spread across his face. He was mad, but pulled himself together and with a quivering voice said, "I have just received a letter from Sam Houston. He feels that the time isn't right and that we could stir up the Indians. There are those around who have told him I have plotted an attack on some friendly Indians. This isn't true, but orders are orders, so I will disband the company as of right now. I thank all of you for joining me. I know it was hard for you to leave your families," he said with his voice still quivering.

The men, all grumbling to each other, started leaving for their homes in groups of twos and threes. He, Joseph, and Nathaniel moved away from the rest of the men.

"What are you going to do now, James?" Nathaniel asked.

"I'm going to check on the Traders to see if they have any new information about the captives. If they don't, I'm going into the Indian Territory and try to find some leads where the tribes are."

"James, I need to head for home. The Illinois Senate will already be in session before I can get there. Unless I can help you, I'm heading home."

"You go on home, Nathaniel. I will go with James for a while before I head for home," Joseph said.

Nathaniel headed home and he and Joseph headed for Coffee's Trading Post that was only a mile away. Nobody at Coffee's had heard any news of the captives. They went to Marshall's Trading Post and none of the traders knew anything about the captives. He was discouraged by this time and said, "I'm heading for the Nation."

"I will go with you," Joseph answered.

They crossed the Red River and traveled from one Indian village to another. He kept asking questions about his daughter, Rachel. The Indians, even if they knew anything, wouldn't answer him. He and Joseph spent three days in a small village when Joseph came down with the fever.

"James, I'm too sick to go any farther. I'm going to head for home."

"Are you sure you can make it home by yourself?"

"Yeah, I'm sorry to have to leave, but I don't feel that good. What are you going to do?"

"I'm going back east and check the villages we missed."

He headed east and Joseph headed back towards the Red River. He entered the second Indian's Village when he saw an Indian wearing a vest. The vest looked from a distance like the one he made a year ago. He headed at an angle to get ahead of the Indian so he could get a better look at the vest. The vest had buttons made out of gourds. There couldn't be two vests made the same way with qourd buttons on it. "Where did you get that vest?"

"I don't know. Someone gave it to me," the Indian replied. James pulled out his knife and cut off one of the buttons. The Indian stood in shock while he examined the button. Yes, it was his vest because he remembered making that button. When he had been sawing the button he had nicked it with the saw. This was his vest; he had made those gourd buttons himself. He mounted his horse, rode a short distance, turned, and shot a new hole through the vest where the button had been. He rode out of the Indian village as fast as his horse would run. He figured he had better get back to Texas in a hurry.

By the time he arrived in Texas, he was sick with the fever. He wanted to go and check the traders along the Red River, but he could barely travel. His fever was terrible. He knew that he would be lucky just to get home. On the way he heard a white woman captive had been ransomed. Since he was too sick with fever to travel back to Coffee's Trading Post, he headed for his son-in-law, Levin Nixon's place.

He arrived at Levin's cabin before sundown and saw Levin coming in from the corn field. He sat down on a stump and waited on him. His shirt was wet with sweat from the fever and he was weak. Levin stopped in front of him and with a shocked look said, "You don't look so good."

"I got myself a case of the fever. I feel like I'm burning all over and I can't get enough water."

"Well, come on back to the well and I will get you a good cool drink and maybe it will help you."

`Levin walked away leaving him sitting on the stump. After three tries, he struggled to pull himself up. Levin had pulled up a bucket of water. James took the bucket, tilted his head back, and poured the water over his head and into his mouth. The cool water on his body cooled him down.

"I thought you were going to drown yourself," Levin said.

"It sure felt good at the time. I came by to ask you a favor. I'm too sick to go back to Coffee's Trading Post; it's on the Red River. I hear that some trader has traded for a white woman captive. I need you to go in my place and check."

"I will be glad to if you can get your daughter to give me permission."

"She will let you go 'cause it could be her sister, "James said.

"My crops are all in good shape and if we can get her permission I will leave in the morning."

* * *

Sarah gave her permission without question. She had never seen her father so sick. She tried to get him to sleep in the house, but he decided the cabin was too hot. He would feel better sleeping in the dog run. At daylight James was awake when Levin came out of the house carrying two small bags. Levin saddled his horse and tied the bags together behind the saddle. Levin mounted, waved good-by to James and Sarah, and rode off north.

Sarah gave James his breakfast and when he had finished, he saddled his horse. Sarah begged James to stay until he felt better, but he knew he would feel better at home.

* * *

Meanwhile, Levin wasn't sure of the location of Coffee's Trading Post. James had just said to follow the road up to the Red River and go west until he saw it. He had left Nacogdoches that morning and was riding in the shade of the pine, oak, and green elms that lined the road. He was ready to cross a small stream, but decided to get a drink of water first. He was letting his horse drink when a man rode up on the other side.

"She is a hot one today, ain't she?"

"Yes, it is. How far is it to the Red River?" he asked moving more into the shade.

"It will take you a good seven days unless you want to kill your horse. I'm Glen Parks, I live near Houston."

"I'm Levin Nixon."

"Aren't you relation to James Parker?"

"Yeah, he's my father-in-law. He's too sick, so I'm going to Coffee's on the red for him."

"I heard some news you might be interested in. I heard a Rachel Plummer was ransomed by a Colonel William Donoho, a trader in Santa Fe. He's bringing her to Independence with his family."

"Well, it looks like I will be heading to that ... Independece. Where is it located?"

"I'm not sure. It's somewhere straight north of here I think. I have never been there, but if you follow this road till you come to a fork, take the left fork. The left fork will take you to the Jonesboro crossing. You can cross the Red River there and you will be in the Indian Territory."

"Would you do me a favor and stop at James' house and tell him that I'm going to Independence to pick up Rachel, and he will have to take care of Sarah and the kids."

"I will be more than happy to do it."

He crossed the creek, and as he rode away, turned in his saddle, waved back at Parks, and pushed his horse into a fast trot. Two hours later he came to the fork in the road. He wasn't sure which fork to take, but decided on the left fork. The road crossed the Red River and headed north. Since Independence was north, he figured he was heading in the right direction.

After five days on the road he was beginning to wonder if he was headed in the right direction, when he met a man on horseback coming towards him.

"Is this the way to Independence?" he asked.

"Yeah, but she's a far distance from here," the man said. "You just follow this road. It leads right to her."

The man never stopped, just kept on riding. He sat there in the saddle and watched the man ride away. Not a very friendly sort, he thought, as he rode up the road. Ten days later he entered Independence and was surprised at its' size. He was amazed at the two tallest buildings; they had to be churches as both had a cross on top. One was at one end of main street and the other was on the other end. The street was filled with people, stores lining both sides of the street. He had never seen a sight like it. There were hardware, harness, dry-goods, and a food emporium store. He looked at the goods in the emporium. They had smoked and pickled meats, sugar, flour, and vegetables in jars.

He selected some pickled meat, and as he was paying the man, asked, "Do you know where I could find Colonel William Donoho?"

"Well, as far as I know the Colonel hasn't come back from Santa Fe yet, but I hear he's on his way. I can tell you where his house is. You go down to the east end of main street to the church and turn south. His house is in that group. He has a sign out in front with his name on it, but nobody has lived in it for a year or so."

He got on his horse, rode out to find the Colonel's house. After turning at the church he saw the houses. There must have been one-hundred one-story clapboard houses. All were whitewashed. He rode back and forth between the rows of houses until he found the Colonel's house. He decided to ride on south and found a place where there was a spring and good grass for his horse.

Every day he rode up and checked to see if the Colonel was home. On the third day he went back to the emporium and purchased some more pickled meat. On his way back he saw a wagon half unloaded in front of the house. He knocked on the door and Rachel opened it.

"Levin, is it really you?" she asked, giving him a big hug."How did you know I was here?"

"Mr. Parks told me, and James was sick, so I came after you."

"Levin, this is Colonel Donoho and his wife who have befriended me. Without their help, I don't think I would have made it."

"When can you be ready to leave?" he asked.

"She needs a couple of days rest before she leaves. The trip up here was no picnic for her or me," the Colonel's wife said.

He moved from the spring and stayed with the Colonel for the next two days. He purchased a horse for Rachel and the Colonel's wife gave him one of her old side saddles. They left early in the morning and rode for about three hours.

"Levin, we need to stop, I need to talk to you."

"We can stop here as good as any place."

"You haven't said one word about James Platt."

"He's still a captive, also; as well as John and Cynthia Ann."

"Levin, I can't go back to Texas, I need to go some place where no one knows me. I know how people look at people like me who has lived with Indians. I know the Colonel's wife was trying to be nice, by giving me her side saddle. I would hate to think how many miles I have ridden bareback."

"Yes, but what about your family? They will be happy to see you."

"You know they will be polite, but behind my back they will make fun of me with their friends. I have seen it happen before and I don't want any part of it."

"Rachel, come home with me, and I promise that we will help you disappear, but you have to go see your family first."

"OK, but remember, I almost killed an Indian with a club so you had better make good your promise, Levin, because I have nothing to lose."

Chapter 18

HORSE CREEK AFFLUENCE OF CANADIAN RIVER IN OLDHAM COUNTY.

SEPTEMBER 16, 1837

Naduah went hunting everyday with Peta. There were many small herds of buffalo grazing in the valley. She was tired of loading meat in the morning, spending the afternoon cutting up the meat into strips to dry. Sometimes she would go to sleep before the sunset. She was awakened from a sound sleep by the yelling. She knew that someone was trying to steal the horses. It was almost daylight and braves came running past her tepee heading to where the horses were grazing. She started to run with them when she heard Gray Foot yell.

"Naduah, stop! Stay in camp where you will be safe."

"What if they steal paint?"

"If they steal Paint, Peta will give you a new horse, but if they capture you, your life could be very hard."

Gray Foot finally got her stripping meat, but her mind wasn't on her work. All she could think about was what if they stole Paint, or what if Peta would get hurt. She had seen him run by near the front of the group. She was having all kinds of crazy thoughts when she saw Little Foot walking back from where the horses grazed.

"Little Foot, did they get Paint?"

"No! Peta is riding him. We found him with a few strays, but there wasn't enough horses for all of us."

"Who is with him?"

"High Wolf is leading the group."

She felt better knowing that High Wolf was with Peta because he was one of the few Chiefs that only attacked when the odds were in his favor. She couldn't keep her mind on the job of stripping meat, and wished that Gray Foot would stop yelling at her.

* * *

High Wolf didn't try to catch up with the raiding party. He knew they were Cheyenne and their main camp was three days north of the Arkansas River. He led the braves in a northeasterly direction into the low ground of Rita Blanca Creek. He knew that Rita Blanca ran in a northwesterly direction, hoping to cross their trail before the Cheyenne camp. He stopped the braves at the confluence of Carrizo Creek.

"We will rest here for a while because we have a big night ahead of us."

* * *

Peta looked at Little Bear, started to say something, but saw High Wolf's eyes watching all their reactions. He had just started to hobble Paint so he could graze when he saw High Wolf walking towards him.

"I want you to take a little ride with me while the others rest," High Wolf said in a low voice. Not even waiting for an answer, turned and walked away.

He was shocked, hurried and removed the hobble and mounted Paint.

"Where are you going?" Little Bear asked as Peta rode past.

"I don't know, but I will tell you when I get back."

He rode to the outer edge of the campsite and saw High Wolf waiting for him. Without a word, High Wolf kicked his horse into a very hard pace. Paint, on his own, picked up the pace and both horses were running like they had rested all day.

After a while High Wolf pulled his horse to a walk and Paint slowed on his own. He turned into an arroyo; it was dry and had a gravel bottom. The arroyo turned west, and ahead Peta could see a butte rising abruptly. He still wasn't sure what they were doing, or why they were there. They kept riding straight for the butte until they came to a level place, halfway up the sloping side. High Wolf dismounted and started to hobble his horse, so he did the same.

When High Wolf started walking on up the slope, he followed. Near the top High Wolf stopped and squatted down. Peta started to say something, but High Wolf stopped him by placing his hand on his mouth gently. High Wolf motioned Peta to follow him as he deliberately worked his way on up the slope. When they arrived at the top High Wolf again stopped and listened. Then crept up until he could see over the top of the flat butte.

100

They could see the cloud of dust created by the horse herd. High Wolf showed the dust to Peta; they moved quickly back down the slope to the horses.

"Peta, I want you to ride along the bottom of the butte every so often to check and see if there is dust from the horse herd. Do not go on top of the butte because the Cheyenne have scouts watching their back trail. They will stop before sundown when they are sure no one is following. When you are sure they have stopped, that will be a ways north of here; make sure that they are camped and then come to find us. We will be camped on Rita Blanca."

* * *

Peta, now alone and scared, watched High Wolf who mounted his horse and rode away. This was the first time he had ever been left by himself. He mounted Paint and headed around the buttes. The sun was hot after passing the first butte. He saw ahead a mountain rising above the plains. The plains provided good cover for him as he worked his way through the pinon thickets.

He came upon an arroyo which ran between the buttes. After looking it over and decided it would provide him cover, he rode into the arroyo which would lead him to the crest of the butte. He was able again to see the dust rising from the horse herd, but realized that the herd was moving faster than he was. He raced Paint as hard as the condition of the terrain would allow. There was an opening between the buttes, and he could see a mountain rising to the sky. The only cover between him and the horse herd was the pinon tree and bushes. If High Wolf was right, and the Cheyenne had left a warrior to watch their back trail, would they be watching here?

He stopped, watched, and listened for something out of place. There were very few birds in the area. He hadn't seen any animals or movement. If he only knew how far it was to the Rita Blanca. The sun was going down behind the mountain; they should make camp soon. He decided to make a run for it. If they left guards behind, he hoped Paint could out run them.

Paint laid his ears back and ran flat out. In a short time he was out of the plains. He let Paint rest by walking him. Now, he could again see the dust from the herd ahead of him. Descending the mesa he was surprised to find a creek at the bottom. It had to be the Rita Blanca Creek. He stopped and studied the area because it would be after dark when he returned.

He let Paint get a drink out of the creek and graze a little along the bank. Starting again he let Paint pick his own speed but felt he was still farther behind the herd. He pushed Paint harder. They had been going up a slope and he could see a mesa ahead. He slowed Paint down. He was almost at the crest when he saw the dust on his left. He had made up a lot of time so he stopped, dismounted Paint and walked, keeping the dust in sight.

The sun was down and the dust was hard to see, then the dust seemed to disappear. Leaving Paint, he worked his way over the west side of the mesa where he could look into the valley below. He saw a river ahead and the Indians camp and the horse herd grazing along the Cimarron. It was getting dark. The moon hadn't risen yet as he retraced his route back to Rita Blanca. He reached the Rita Blanca and remembered what High Wolf told him to do. He howled like a coyote and got three answers back. Which direction should he go? The one came from the south, so that wasn't High Wolf, and the one from the west couldn't be, so he turned east; then the coyote howled again from the east. Peta answered back and kept moving down stream when out of the brush moved High Wolf.

Peta was tired. Seemed like it took him forever to get back to the camp. He turned Paint loose with the rest of the horses and went to the fire where a deer was cooking. Cutting off a big chunk of meat, he sat down on the ground. High Wolf came and sat with him as he ate. Peta drew the location of the Cheyenne Camp on the ground.

High Wolf studied the map for a while and said, "Peta, I am going to give you four braves. You will lead them, following the Rita Blanca Creek until you cross the trail the herd used. Wait there until another warrior joins you. Very slowly follow the tracks of the herd toward the Cheyenne Camp until you meet the horses running toward you. Then spread out. You will take the lead and have your braves drive the herd home, pushing the herd hard until you have crossed the Rita Blanca. You can then slow them down. The rest of us will catch up with you."

High Wolf stood, gave him a hard look, turned and walked away. The camp became alive, everyone was preparing to leave. He sat quietly, finished eating, then went and caught Paint. When he returned to camp there were four braves waiting for him. He led the group like High Wolf had directed. The group was starting to get restless.

He heard the click of a horse's hoof on the rocky creek bed. Peta motioned the braves to spread out while he waited for the horseman to appear. It was Little Bear. He motioned for the group to follow.

* * *

102

When High Wolf's group reached the Cimarron River, he motioned the group to spread out leaving their horses with two braves. The braves that left the group along the way were now rejoining High Wolf's group. They had killed all the guards guarding the back trail. The Cheyenne camp was quiet, having no idea that the Comanche had killed and scalped all the camp guards. High Wolf's braves now completely surrounded the camp and were waiting for a signal. The Comanche-yell filled the air, a high-pitched, blood-chilling cry that struck terror in every enemy.

The herd of horses, both Cheyenne and Comanche, broke into a dead run south of the camp with four Comanche waving Cheyenne blankets at them. The attack had started and was over in a few minutes. The Comanche were going wild, scalping and gathering up their booty.

* * *

Peta's group, who were still some distance away, heard the Comanche-yell and the thundering sound of running horses. Peta motioned for his braves to spread out and he swung in front of the lead horse. Star was leading the horses. Peta moved Paint closer to Star. Peta pulled up his right leg to force Paint in tight against Star. Peta switched horses. Now, on Star, he let them run. After they crossed the Rita Blanca, Peta started slowing the horse down as it was still a long way home to the Canadian River.

* * *

The sun was coming up when High Wolf and the rest of the braves joined them. High Wolf's group was loaded down with plunder. He decided to let the braves rest on Carrizo Creek. The braves needed some of the horses for pack animals to carry all their loot. Each of his braves had three to four scalps tied onto their lance. He watched as the braves picked out horses for pack animals. When he saw that everyone had their loot packed on horses, he led them into Carrizo Creek and followed it down to Rita Blanca.

They arrived on the Canadian River at sundown where they made camp. The booty was piled together away from the campfire. High Wolf went to the pile and selected a Cheyenne blanket. After all the older braves had their pick, he nodded to Peta. Rising and walking to the pile, Peta selected a blanket as it would be his gift to Naduah. After the last warrior had chosen one article from the pile, High Wolf's group kept taking turns choosing items until the pile was gone.

The next morning at sunrise everyone made himself look the best he could, then pulled grass and rubbed their horses down. Since they didn't have their war bag, they couldn't put on war paint. High Wolf sent one of the young braves to their camp with the news that the raiding party had returned, and to line up in the camp because he was driving the horse herd through. He led the braves toward the camp. They could hear the women singing. The braves had cleaned their lances and tied the scalps with colorful strips of cloth.

* * *

Peta followed behind with the horse herd, riding Star with Paint trotting along side. The people lined the wide passageway to keep the horses together. He saw Naduah and Gray Foot together singing. He smiled at her and she smiled back. Gray Foot just waved and laughed at them both. Later that afternoon he came to Gray Foot's tepee carrying a Cheyenne blanket. Gray Foot was packing dry buffalo strips into a bag. When she saw him she smiled and said, "Oh! how good of you to bring me such a pretty Cheyenne blanket."

"It's ... it's for Naduah," Peta replied with a surprised look on his face, then felt bad.

"You know I almost guessed that."

"Here, you take the blanket and I will give Naduah a horse.

High Wolf gave me five more horses than he gave the rest of the braves," throwing out his chest.

"No, you give her the blanket and the horse because she keeps more things than I do. That way she will have her own pack horse."

"OK, but where is she, anyway?"

"She went to the spring to get some fresh water. Horse Creek water tastes as bad as the Canadian River."

"I have to go tell her that the blanket is for her, and I am giving her a mare as a pack horse. With luck, she can raise a colt." Peta turned and left, leaving Gray Foot standing there shaking her head. What was she to do with those two?

Chapter 19

PRAIRIE DOG TOWN FORK OF THE RED RIVER IN PALO DURO CANYON.

MAY 5, 1840

Naduah was amazed at the sight of the canyon. The steep colored walls of pink, green, mauve, buff, and yellow, looked like they rose to the sky. The tall junipers, red cedars, hackberry, and mesquite covered the floor. Gray Foot had to keep yelling at her because she would stop helping her put up the tepee. Naduah's thoughts turned from the canyon's beauty to Peta as she hadn't seen him since they arrived.

* * *

Peta went straight to Iron Shirt who was standing in the shade of a tree watching his wives put up his big tepee.

"What do you want? You only come around when you want or need something."

"I would like to marry Naduah."

"Is she ready to marry you?"

"I don't know? But I think she is."

"I will talk to Gray Foot and see if she is ready. Then I will let you know. How many horses do you have?"

"Fifty-sixty, why do you ask?"

"If she is ready to marry, then you are going to give Gray Foot fifty horses. You can keep ten of your best."

"But why? She is mine; I captured her."

"Because I said so. I want the camp to know, as her quardian, that not many braves your age can afford her. I will see Gray Foot today and ask her. She will make the decision."

Peta started to say something more, but the look on Iron Shirt's face told him he it was better left alone.

* * *

Iron Shirt went to Gray Foot's tepee. Naduah was away gathering firewood, so he and Gray Foot could talk.

"Peta asked if he could marry Naduah. What do you think about it? Is she ready?"

"Yes, she is ready as she has learned our ways and also our language, but I sure hate to lose her. She helps me with everything and is the best of company. I will surely miss her."

"Since Peta has Sensa, I will tell him that Naduah will still help you. For this, in return, you will give back half of the horse herd that he is to give you."

"Thank you, my son. You don't know how happy that makes me."

He turned and walked away smiling to himself, because he did know how much Gray Foot had become attached to Naduah.

* * *

Peta had been watching Iron Shirt so he waited until he reached his tepee. He tried to act casual as he walked past Iron Shirt. Iron Shirt sat outside of his tepee and acted like he never saw him. He walked on down a ways, but he couldn't take it any longer, he turned and came back.

"I thought you had changed your mind about wanting to marry Naduah, since you just walked on by without asking.

"I was scared to ask, afraid you would say no."

"I have new rules that you have to agree to. She is still to help Gray Foot and for this Gray Foot will give you back half of your horses. Naduah, young and white, isn't broken in yet. I expect for you to be gentle with her and treat her good. If I hear differently, you have me to deal with."

"I agree," he said with a big smile on his face, because just a few minutes ago, after looking at Iron Shirt's face, he thought the answer was no.

He hurried through the camp looking for Little Foot and Little Bear. He found Little Bear who led him to where Little Foot was.

"I have a big favor to ask both of you. I have received permission from Iron Shirt to marry Naduah. I need you two to take fifty horses to Gray Foot's tepee. Hold them there until Gray Foot and Naduah make their move. Then help drive them back to my horse herd or to theirs. Now, I will go with you and help get the horses."

* * *

When Naduah returned Gray Foot said, "Iron Shirt gave Peta permission to marry you. You will live with him at night but will still help me in the day time. Peta will have someone drive fifty horses here to my tepee. When I drive the horses into my herd then you are married to Peta."

She was happy about marrying Peta, but she hated to leave Gray Foot. She felt better after hearing the arrangement. She could hardly work as she kept watching for the horses. Gray Foot just kept on working like it was an everyday occurrence. When Little Bear and Little Foot drove Peta's horses to the tepee, she could hardly hold herself back. Why doesn't Gray Foot make an effort that she was accepting the horses. Little Bear and Little Foot aren't sure if Gray Foot was keeping the horses or returning the horses. Eventually, Gray Foot motioned to her to help drive the horses. She saw that Little Bear and Little Foot were going to help them. She and Gray Foot took the lead and the horses followed them to the herd.

When they returned, Peta was at Gray Foot's tepee. He had come to help her pack and move. She was both happy and sad while she was packing. When they were ready to leave, she hugged Gray Foot and started to cry. Gray Foot, like the true Comanche she was, held it well, but there were traces of water in her eyes.

She knew that Sensa didn't take the new arrangement very well. She was no longer boss of Peta's tepee-just a slave with a new boss. Peta in no uncertain words told her so. She was scared of Sensa and her black raven eyes sent shivers up and down her spine. She spent the rest of the day trying to stay out of Sensa's way. She moved her bed to the opposite side of the tepee. When Peta came home he crawled in bed with her.

She could feel the heat of his body next to hers as she was turned away facing the tepee. He then put his arm around her and pulled her close. This was the first time she had slept with anyone since she was a little girl. Peta started rubbing her shoulder, then down her body until he reached her butt. She was burning up all over. He stopped and was sound asleep with his hand laying on her butt.

107

When she awoke at sunrise he was gone. How she hated to get up and face Sensa. Then she remembered that she was to go and help Gray Foot, so she hurried out of the tepee while Sensa was still asleep. Gray Foot was up and had a good fire going by the time she arrived.

"Well, how is married life?"

"Very different, yes, very different."

She gathered firewood and carried water for Gray Foot all morning. Around noon a new band of Comanche moved in next to the Noconis. Gray Foot told her that they were Quahadas Comanche also, but their Chief's name was Wild Horse. She decided since she didn't want to go back to Peta's tepee and face Sensa, she would gather more firewood. She was walking down an old animal path, not looking for firewood, when she met a warrior younger than herself coming towards her. She kept looking at him. There was something familiar about him. She had seen him before. Was it her brother, John? As they passed each other, she turned and said, "John, is that you?"

He stopped. He couldn't believe his ears. Was this Cynthia Ann? No, Cynthia Ann wouldn't look like that. He turned around and took a real good hard look at her.

"Is that you, Cynthia Ann?"

"Yes, John, it's me. You sure have grown a lot since I last saw you five years ago."

"We both have. You are the best looking squaw I have ever seen."

"I'm married now, got married yesterday. I married a good kind warrior. His father is our Chief Iron Shirt."

"I hope to become a warrior this year."

"Have you seen any of the others?" Cynthia Ann asked.

"Yes, about three moons ago I saw James Platt. He's with Chief Shaking Hands band of the Kotsatekas tribe. Chief Shaking Hands has raised him and calls him Toniet because he can run like a deer."

"How about Rachel? I haven't her since we separated."

"I heard she is with the Yamparikas tribe, but I have never seen her," John said.

"Come, let me take you to my Indian mother. I think without her I would have died. She is my husband's grandmother and the mother of Iron Shirt. You will like her."

Naduah led off back down the trail with John following her. Gray Foot was roasting meat over the fire. Naduah told how she met John, her brother. Since both Naduah and John could speak in Comanche, Gray Foot sat and listened while they all ate the fresh roasted meat.

* * *

Peta saw Naduah return with a new warrior. He hurried to Gray Foot's tepee to see who this new warrior was. Why was his new wife and Gray Foot giving him so much attention. Peta was a little hard when he arrived. But as soon as Naduah told him who John was, he led him all over camp, telling everyone he met that he was her brother. His new name was White Wolf, and he was in Wild Horse's band. When they came back she asked him if she and White Wolf could go riding. Peta agreed, if he could go with them. Naduah was more than happy because they hadn't ridden together for a long time.

He left the tepee early the next morning but told her that he would bring Paint to Gray Foot's tepee. Then they would ride over to Wild Horse's camp and pick up Little Wolf. She was so happy her brother was here and Peta seemed to like him. She had just finished gathering the wood and carrying water for Gray Foot when Peta arrived. She ran up to Paint and gave him a hug and started rubbing his neck.

"She thinks more of that horse than she does of me, he said with a little laugh.

"Just wait till the cold weather comes, you will see how much she loves you then," Gray Foot said with a big smile on her face.

"I can't wait for winter," Peta replied as he watched Naduah mount Paint and they rode off together. Gray Foot just stood there shaking her head watching them ride away.

When they arrived at Chief Wild Horse's camp, it was a quieter camp than Iron Shirt's. There were very few people moving around. Little Wolf was watching for them and waved. He was standing with Chief Wild Horse and introduced them both.

Peta told Wild Horse he had heard a lot about him from his father Iron Shirt and felt like he already knew him. Wild Horse laughed and said,

"Your father and I have been friends for many seasons. He is a good Comanche and has never befriended any Comanche band. He is an honorable man. I hope when you take his place you can fill his moccasins."

Peta just stared at the ground and it was Naduah that broke the silence.

"Peta has become a good hunter and has many horses in his herd. Now that we are married we will have a son who some day will be Chief as good as his father and his grandfather."

Peta's face turned red and was lost for words. It was Little Wolf who came to his rescue when he said, "That's a tall order for a white Comanche to say."

Peta was beginning to understand his new wife. She may be white but she thought like a Comanche. Who could ask for anything more. As they rode back to Iron Shirt's camp Little Wolf told them that Wild Horse was leaving in the morning. The Comancheros were in Yellow House Canyon which was one of the reasons they moved into the area. They had many buffalo hide to trade.

Chapter 20

CLEAR FORK OF THE BRAZOS IN THROCKMORTON COUNTY, TEXAS.

NOVEMBER, 1842

John Parker, known as Little Wolf, was now thirteen years old. He had proven himself to be a good hunter. Now, he was waiting for a chance to go on a raid in hopes of becoming a warrior. His Indian father was Chief Wild Horse. The band had camped for the winter. The band loved antelope, not only the taste, but chase. The antelopes were light on their feet and could change direction instantly. Sometimes the chase not only wore out the antelope but also the Indian pony.

Little Wolf saw a crowd around Chief Wild Horse's tepee; then he recognized the Indian agent, Archer Wheeler. He wasn't concerned with the goings on at Wild Horse's tepee, and headed for the pasture to check one of his horses. His favorite horse had come up lame while hunting. He caught his horse and started rubbing his leg and found his knee was swollen. Little Wolf led him over to the creek and started packing the horse's leg with mud.

"Little Wolf! Chief Wild Horse needs you at his tepee now."

Little Wolf didn't return an answer but hurried off to Chief Wild Horse. When he arrived the crowd moved back to let him through. Chief Wild Horse and Agent Wheeler were talking in sign language. Chief Wild Horse looked up and saw Little Wolf standing in front of the crowd and said in Comanche.

"Little Wolf, I have just traded you for seventy-five dollars of goods that the band needs. You have been a good son and served me and the band well. It's with great sadness that I must tell you this. I have also promised that you will not run away. I wish it could be different."

Little Wolf felt like crying but knew the whole camp was watching, so he took it like the young warrior he was. The world that he had come to love was disappearing before his very eyes. Little Wolf ducked his head and stood there looking at the ground. One of the braves had brought his other horse for him. Agent Wheeler led him away from the camp; they mounted their horses and rode away.

He knew if Chief Shaking Hands hadn't promised Agent Wheeler, he would be back in camp by the next morning. While they rode he promised himself that he would return someway. There were many times that he could have slipped away but didn't. They rode north for about two hours before coming to Millers Creek where it flowed into the Brazos.

There he saw Chief Shaking Hands band of the Kotsatekas Comanche were camped there. Chief Shaking Hands welcomed them and gave them something to eat. Chief Shaking Hands' wives had pieces of buffalo meat roasting over the fire. They spent the night as guests of Chief Shaking Hands. The next morning, when they were ready to leave, Chief Shaking Hands brought a young Indian boy on a small Indian pony. John recognized James Platt Plummer right away because he had seen him only five months ago.

He knew that James Platt wasn't happy about leaving his Indian father, Chief Shaking Hands. Seeing James was trying hard not to cry because Indian boys don't cry, he started talking to him in Comanche. James Platt becomes less afraid and started answering him back.

He realized that the Indian Agent was treating both of them kindly but just didn't understand their love for the Comanche way of life. They were raised as sons of Chiefs and in the Comanche society there was no higher honor. They arrived on the sixth day at Fort Gibson.

* * *

James Platt was scared of the soldiers because they all dressed and look alike. Once inside the fort he ran and hid and it was John and Sergeant Dulaney who found him hiding between some barrels. It was hard to believe that he could squeeze himself between the barrels. John tried talking to him in Comanche but nothing he said worked. After an hour or so Sergeant Dulaney left but came right back with some jujubes. Reaching over the barrels the Sergeant dropped the jujubes down almost on his head and a few landed in his lap.

He had never seen any jujubes before but like all curious little boys they found their way into his mouth. After he had moved around and picked up all Sergeant Dulaney dropped, he looked up at the Sergeant. Not saying a word, the Sergeant reached into his pocket, took out a small handful and placed them on top of the outside barrel. If he wanted any more, he would have to crawl to get them.

He watched the Sergeant grab John by the arm and led him across the yard where they sat down on some kegs. He started moving around, trying to work his way out. He crept out, peeking over the barrel to make sure it was all right. When he felt safe, he rushed over to the jujubes and hogged them down.

After he put the last one in his mouth, the Sergeant stood up and placed three more jujubes on the keg. Taking a hold of John's arm, hurried him around the corner of the building. When he looked around the corner of the building to see where they were, he saw Sergeant hand John his first piece of candy. The Sergeant started to reach into his pocket to get another jujube when James Platt came running over. The Sergeant handed the candy to John and James Platt looked for a minute like he was going to fight. The Sergeant, reaching back into his pocket, handed a jujube to him. He and the Sergeant became good friends. Everywhere the Sergeant went he followed for jujubes.

* * *

James Parker read in the newspaper about two white boys ransomed at Fort Gibson. He left the next day, arriving at Fort Gibson twenty-two days later. Seven years had passed since the raid on Fort Parker. The Commandant Captain Brown of Fort Gibson greeted him. After hearing his story, Captain Brown called Sergeant Dulaney to bring the boys for him to identify. He recognized John without question, but James Platt had changed more. He still had his mother Rachel's face so James identified them both.

Captain Brown filled out the necessary papers charging Sam Houston, President of Republic of Texas, for the $150.00 to be paid to the United States for the two boys. He also filled out a legal form for James to sign as their legal guardian until such time they could be returned to their parents.

Captain Brown called for Sergeant Dulaney to turn the boys over to him. When the Sergeant returned with the boys, James Platt found out James was taking them away; he ran away and hid. Sergeant Dulaney, good with sign language, talked to John and he repeated it to James Platt in Comanche. John and the Sergeant finally convinced James Platt that he should go with John and James. The Sergeant handed John a sack of jujubes and told John to give one to James Platt every so often. James took John to his mother's place and Lucy was overjoyed with John's return.

***

113

John, however, wished that he was back with the Comanche. He had a very hard time talking to his mother, Lucy, because she knew no Comanche, not even signs. He had forgotten his English. What he did remember, he said with a Comanche accent that his mother couldn't understand.

He kept stealing a horse and running away but he was always caught and brought back. Finally, he had learned enough English that he persuaded his mother Lucy to let him return and he would bring Cynthia Ann home. She agreed and gave him a good horse. He headed for the Pease River there he found Iron Shirt's band camped on the Pease. He talked to Naduah for over a week trying to persuade her to return with him to their mother.

Naduah explained to him that she was now married. She was happy with her husband and her life. She wouldn't leave his love for anything or anybody. After talking to Naduah, he realized that he, too, missed the Comanche way of life. The next day he told Naduah that he was returning to Wild Horse.

Chapter 21

WICHITA RIVER IN BAYLOR COUNTY TEXAS.

SEPTEMBER, 1844

John rode toward Wild Horse's tepee and everyone who saw him followed along behind. Wild Horse saw the crowd coming and recognized Little Wolf. Little Wolf dismounted and led his horse in front of Wild Horse's tepee.

"Wild Horse, my mother gave me permission to return to the Comanche; I didn't escape. I'm supposed to talk my sister Naduah into returning to our mother. She said she isn't leaving the Noconis. I wish to rejoin your band and become a great warrior."

"My son, you don't know how happy I am to see you back. After you left I was sorry I traded you. I will never make that mistake again and I will see that you get a chance to become a warrior."

Little Wolf spent the next week going on hunting parties. The camp honored him for returning to them. He knew it was the time of the year for the "Mexican Moon" when the full moon would shine almost like daylight. The Mexicans called it the "Comanche Moon" because the Comanche raid the most during this time. Little Wolf had just returned from hunting and Wild Horse sent for him to come to his tepee.

Little Wolf hurried off but worried to hear what Wild Horse wanted. When he arrived Wild Horse was standing in front of his tepee talking to White Bear.

"White Bear is going on a raid into Mexico and I have asked him to take you along. If you do good on the raid, I will hold a warrior dance for you to show the whole camp your courage by returning to us and completing your first raid."

"I will make you proud of me, my father."

At sundown the war party gathered at the west end of the camp and paraded around the camp several times. When darkness fell upon the camp, the big fire in the center of the camp provided light for their war dance. Around midnight the leader left the dance followed by the braves.

They picked up their weapons, food, and clothing, and headed for the appointed rendezvous. Little Wolf went to Wild Horse's tepee where Walk Around, Wild Horse's wife, fixed him a war bag and a bow with many arrows. When he was traded, the camp split his property among themselves. White Bear's raiding party would leave in the dark because it was bad medicine to leave in the daylight.

They traveled for four days down the Comanche Trail before crossing the Rio Grande River. They followed the River Conchos to the Spanish City of Chihuahua. Their main purpose was to capture Spanish horses and any women or children. Chihuahua was surrounded by ranchos with many fine Spanish horses. The owner had them all in corrals with only one or two guards.

The raiding party split into four groups. The groups would all be in place ready to kill the guards at a signal from White Bear. Since the sound would be coming from four different areas, the Mexicans wouldn't know which way to go. Some would stay with their own herds and family, because when the Comanche hit no one was safe.

Little Wolf was slow in working his way towards the corral. He had lost contact with his group when the signal came. He started running and as he turned the corner of the hacienda, he ran into a girl. They hit the ground, with Little Wolf lying on top of her. By now the whole area was in an uproar, people running everywhere. It was time to get out of there. Little Wolf was bigger, but she was stronger. Finally, he grabbed her by the hair and dragged her to his horse.

After four attempts he succeeded in getting her on his horse. Holding one of her legs, he reached under the horse and tied her feet with rawhide. Now, if she tried to get off, she could ride upside down with her head dragging on the ground. He and the girl joined the raiding party. The rest of the group had captured many horses. He needed horses but capturing the young girl satisfied him. They rode for two hours. After they were sure no one was chasing them, they stopped to rest.

He left his captive tied up on the ground and walked over to White Bear and asked, "Could I have a horse? If we keep up this pace my horse will not make it carrying the both of us."

"Cut one out of the herd," White Bear said not even looking up.

"Untie me. I will not run away. I have been watching the other captives and how they are being mistreated. I will do you no dishonor." She spoke in Spanish, but he knew enough Spanish words he understood her, so he untied her.

116

The group traveled for three more days. Around noon they stopped to let the horses have their fill of grass and water. Little Wolf had been burning hot for two days and now he was breaking out with pox. White Bear saw him and yelled,

"He has smallpox! I have seen it before. Leave him or we all will die from this white man's disease."

Little Wolf was sick. He was happy they left him lying on the ground. He must have gone to sleep because when he awoke it was dark and the Comanche Moon lit the area. Moving slowly he moved over to the water, washed his face, took a big drink, laid back, and went to sleep. When he awoke someone was feeling his forehead.

"Who are you?"

"It's me, Donna, your captive."

"What are you doing here?"

"Well, you captured me so I am yours and I like you."

"How did you get here?"

"Well, I slipped off, stole two horses, and just rode back. If you don't want me, I can leave you and ride on home."

"I'm sorry, I just can't believe you would come back to help me."

"You don't have to worry. They aren't going to be coming after me. White Bear is scared and I think that's the reason it was so easy for me to escape. He was afraid you made me sick, also."

"Well, I'm taking you back home."

"I don't want to go home. I want to stay with you, and if I take you home, they could kill you."

"Ok, we will go and join a Comanche band in Mexico. I have met some of them."

"I didn't know there were Comanche living in Mexico."

"It happened about three years ago. President Lamar of Texas sent Colonel John Moore with Rangers and Lipan scouts to teach the Comanche a lesson. They came up on a band of Penatekas Comanche camped on the river. The Colonel attacked the camp at dawn with orders to shoot anything that moved. They killed most of the chiefs, many women and children. Afterward, the bands split. Some went north across the Red River, and the others went south below the Rio Grande River."

"Will they accept us?"

117

"I hope so, cause we don't have much choice right now."

He wasn't sure where to look for the Comanche. They headed back across the Rio Grande River, then headed toward the mountains. The last time he heard they were living in the mountains but which ones, he didn't know. They traveled until sunset and were at the foothill of a mountain.

He opened his war bag. Walk Around had filled it with dried meat, pemmican, flint, and steel. Donna helped him gather the wood for a fire. They both were hungry and sat down by the fire and were eating when a stick cracked behind Little Wolf. He jumped up with his bow in hand ready to shoot. He backed Donna around the fire to the other side and they waited.

The night was silent-no sounds from any direction. Then out of the shadows appeared the biggest warrior Little Wolf had ever seen. Donna had moved from behind Little Wolf, but when she saw the warrior, she moved behind Little Wolf hugging him and holding him tight. No one said anything. The Big Brave stood looking at them and they stood looking back.

Finally, the Big Brave said, "You Comanche?"

"Yes, I'm Comanche. My name is Little Wolf, son of Wild Horse."

"What are you doing here?"

"We are looking for the Southern Comanche that live around here. This is my Mexican captive and I am looking for a new band to join up with."

"In the morning I will take to Tosaw; he is our chief."

"What is your name?"

"They call me Big Mountain."

"The name fits you." Little Wolf said.

"Do you want something to eat?"

"I'd take a piece of that pemmican."

"Here, help yourself," and handed him all that was left and Big Mountain took it all. They broke camp at daylight since Big Mountain was afoot. He and Donna walked with him and led their horses. He was surprised at the size of the camp. It was the biggest camp of Comanche together in one place he had ever seen.

Big Mountain led them into the center of the camp to the largest tepee in the camp. Big Mountain explained to Chief Tosaw who they were and what they wanted. The Chief looked them over real good and asked, "Why did they leave their band?"

Before Big Mountain could say anything, Little Wolf said, "We became lost and missed the meeting place. I knew there were Comanche here in Mexico so we crossed back across the River. We were afraid of the Texans by ourselves," Little Wolf said speaking in the Comanche tongue.

Chief Tosaw was impressed with Little Wolf's use of the Comanche language and welcomed them into his band. A crowd had gathered around the Chief's tepee but moved away as he and Donna turned to leave. He wasn't sure where they were going to stay. Walking through the camp he was looking for a place for them and for the horses. He wasn't sure he wanted to turn them loose into their herd.

"You, Little Wolf, stop! I want to talk to you," said a little old woman, shoulders all bent over from the years of hard work. "Little Wolf, I will make you a deal. I have a tepee but I have no one to hunt for me or help me. I'm getting old and I need help as my sons have all died by the pox and raids. If you will hunt for me, I will let you and your woman share my tepee."

"Show me your tepee," Little Wolf said as the old woman led the way. There was no way he was going to turn down a deal like this. He called her "Old Woman" and she liked it. Donna was happy because at least they had a place to live.

Chapter 22

Naduah loved the spring because of the wild flowers. She always remembered the old Shoshone legend that Gray Foot told her: "Wild flower blooms are the footprints of little children who have died and come back to gladden us." This made her feel closer to the flowers this year because she was heavy with child. She couldn't take her eyes off the many shades of colors of the bluebonnets, poppy mallows, and Indian blanket mixed in with the prairie grass waving to her in the breeze.

Naduah walked because Gray foot told her that riding could cause her to have a miscarriage. She was exhausted which made each new step harder than the one before. She felt that she couldn't take another step because her back and feet hurt.

She yelled, "What's happening?"

Gray Foot was ahead of her and looked back and saw that her water had broken. She grabbed a blanket and ran back to her placing the blanket on the ground. She then had her squat next to the blanket.

She wasn't sure of what was happening but knew by squatting she felt better. Before she realized it Gray Foot reached down, pulled, and she screamed. Gray Foot laid the baby down on the blanket and from her belt she pulled out a soft piece of rawhide. Gray Foot tied the umbilical cord, cut it, and with a rag wiped the baby down.

"He's a boy," she said handing the baby to Naduah. "He looks healthy."

Gray Foot left her and returned to her horse. At first Naduah thought that she was leaving. Gray Foot returned with soft rabbit skin and wrapped the baby up and handed him back to Naduah.

"What are you going to name him?"

"Quanah, because of the sweet smell of the flowers," she said, with a big smile on her face.

Gray Foot placed the blanket in the shade of tree. "Here, sit in the shade and rest for while. We can catch up with the band after you have rested."

* * *

When the band stopped to camp on Elm Creek, Peta missed Gray Foot and Naduah and rode back looking for them. When he found them, he saw that he was now a father of a new son. He was so proud that he had a son. He gave away ten horses to people who needed a horse badly. He and Naduah moved into Gray Foot's tepee so that Gray Foot could help her care for Quanah.

* * *

Whenever Naduah could, she took Quanah for a ride. She loved riding in the wild flowers, smelling the fragrance given off by the horse dragging his feet through the flowers. She was riding along not paying any attention to the world around her, only the beauty and smell of the flowers, when she saw an Army Patrol moving toward her. She was farther from her camp than she had realized. Her first thought was to turn around and make a run for it. Since she hadn't fully recovered from giving birth and Quanah didn't need bouncing around, she stopped and watched them slowly ride toward her. She was nervous because the Army was her Peoples' enemy, even if Iron Shirt had signed a treaty. "The Blue coats couldn't be trusted." She had heard Peta say this many times and always he would give a good example.

The six man patrol rode up and stopped, facing her. She sat her horse and glared back at them.

"Sarg, she's white!"

"I can see Corporal Lester. I do have eyes."

"But Sarg, shouldn't we take her back with us?"

"You get those dumb thoughts out of your head and give me a chance to talk to her. You know we are only on a patrol and we aren't to start any trouble with the Indians. I would say if you took her by force that there's a buck out there who would have your scalp on his lance before nightfall."

She didn't understand what they said but knew they were talking about her. She wished she had ridden away but it was too late now. The Sergeant kept talking to her. She answered him in Comanche. Now, he looked puzzled at her.

121

Then he said in Spanish, "Would you like to leave the Comanche and return to your people?"

She only understood a few words of Spanish that she had learned from Sensa. The Sergeant then tried talking to her in sign language. This she understood and answered in sign language.

"No, I am in love with my husband Peta. I have a new son and the Comanche are my people."

"We are sorry to have bothered you," the Sergeant said and waved the patrol around and rode away.

She sat watching them ride back up the slope and released the tight hold she had on Quanah. She didn't realize until then how tight she was holding him. Quanah was still asleep wrapped in the rabbit fur blanket. She turned Paint around and headed back to camp. She would have to tell Peta because someone may have seen her talking to the patrol.

She turned Paint loose and headed for Gray Foot's tepee. She would tell Gray Foot first. Gray Foot was standing by the fire cooking meat.

"Did you have a pleasant ride?"

"Yes, but an Army Patrol found me and asked me to return to my family."

"What did you tell them?"

"That I was happy here with my husband and my family. Should I tell Peta?"

No, not unless he asks. If he does, then tell him everything that happened. Chances are he already knows."

"They spoke a funny language. It sounded like I had heard it before, but I didn't know what the words meant."

"It's been many seasons since you have heard it. You were a very young girl at the time. Look at you; now married and have a son."

She felt better and hurried off to her own tepee. Peta was there. Quanah was wide awake wanting to be fed. She sat down beside Peta and let Quanah nurse. Peta asked how her ride was but didn't say anything about the patrol. Gray Foot was right again about how Peta would react. She felt so lucky to have been raised by Gray Foot. She loved Gray Foot just like she was her mother. Peta, without a word, left. He was always doing that, but she was getting used to it.

She didn't know that High Wolf was planning a raid into Texas just south of Red River. The white settlers were moving into the area. They would be easy picking for women, children, and horses. Peta needed some more horses, and maybe a girl to help Gray Foot. He also needed the glory and the excitement of the raid.

Peta returned and asked her to paint his face and fix his hair. Sensa was to get his war gear ready. Naduah felt honored because it was the first time he hadn't told her to get his war gear ready. She knew he was getting ready for the parade that would start at sundown. The dance started after the parade, and the raiding party would leave around midnight.

Sensa placed his lance outside the tepee and hung his shield on it facing the setting sun. She then packed a small bag of food.

"Can I stay with Gray Foot while you're gone?" she asked with her head bent and a look of embarrassment.

"Yes, she would love that, but don't let her spoil Quanah,"he answered with a smile on his face.

She joined Gray Foot and the other women as they lined the lanes the Raiding Party would ride through in the camp. The party rode through the camp four times before sundown. The fire was burning high in the middle of the camp. She and Gray Foot sat down with the other women in a circle around the fire. The women all started singing their war songs. Peta came for her to dance and she handed Quanah to Gray Foot. She and Peta joined the other dancers.

When the moon was high in the sky the dance stopped. The braves went to their tepee to get their gear and said their good-byes before they left. She felt all alone, like the only ones in the whole world were Quanah and herself, when a voice broke through the cool night air.

"Well, are you coming or are you just going to stand out here all night looking at the moon?" Gray Foot asked, bending over and picking up a small bag that she needed for Quanah.

"I am always scared that something will happen to Peta."

"Peta has good medicine. He will return; you'll see."

"I can't stop worrying about him."

"Come, let's go home. You have Quanah to worry about. Never spend your time worrying about the old, just the young."

Peta had told her they would be back in four days. She had made four marks in the ground next to the tepee. This morning she rubbed the last mark out, so he should return today. Leaving Quanah with Gray Foot, she hurried to get her work done. She carried the water and then gathered firewood. While she was gathering wood she worked her way up the slope where she could see miles south of the camp. She was disappointed because there was no trail dust or anything moving on the flat prairie below.

"He will return, you'll see, so quit worrying."

"If they were coming today, they should be here by now."

"The Raiding Parties back! They are on their way to the camp now," the camp crier yelled riding though the camp.

She grabbed Quanah up and started to run when Gray Foot yelled, "Wait for me? It will be awhile before they get here."

She made Gray Foot walk all the way through the camp so they could be one of the first to see the returning party. She remembered back to the day when she rode in front of Peta as his captive. Peta wasn't in front of the party so he must not have captured a girl. Then she saw him leading a large herd of horses. As Peta rode past her, he looked at her and smiled.

Chapter 23

ANTELOPE HILLS IN ROGER MILLS COUNTY IN OKLAHOMA.
MAY 1858

Naduah was busy taking care of her two sons, Quanah, six, and Pecos, five, and was expecting the third. They were camped north of Antelope Hills on the Canadian River to hunt buffalo. Buffalo hunting was good along the Canadian where many small herds grazed along the river banks. Peta was taking Sensa with him to load the meat on pack horses. Since Gray Foot wasn't feeling well she spent more time with her.

* * *

Gray Foot, now an old woman, knew that she could no longer keep up when the camp moved or do her share of the work. Gray Foot waited until she was sure everyone was asleep and slipped past the night guards and headed for Antelope Hills, as fast as her old arthritic legs could carry her. She then slowly picked her way through the cedar-flecked canyons. The walking wore her out so she stopped and rested on the ground, leaning against the bank.

The warm sun on her wrinkled face woke her. She had no idea how far she was from camp. She looked around and saw her tracks in the deep red-brown soil. She knew that no one would follow her and she could die with the good spirits. She must now continue on her journey to the Happy Hunting Ground because it was the Comanche way. After three tries she managed to stand up and get her sore legs working, slowly picking her way deeper into Antelope Hills. Her only thoughts were of Naduah and how she would take the news. Peta would have to tell her, but how would she react?

* * *

Naduah went to Gray Foot's tepee and found her gone, but didn't think anything about it. As she left she noticed the fire was out and there

125

was no wood. Gray Foot must have left to gather more wood she thought returning to her own tepee. She helped Sensa cut up meat until the sun was high in the sky. She decided it would be cooler picking up wood for Gray Foot under the Pichot Junipers.

She returned to Gray Foot's tepee and found no fire, no wood, and no Gray Foot. She returned to her own tepee.

"Peta, have you seen Gray Foot this morning?"

"No, but don't worry about her, she will be happy. She has left for the Happy Hunting Ground."

"Then I will find her and bring her back."

"Naduah, she is Comanche. You must let her die like a Comanche. The old man or woman who can't make our next camp or will starve before the next thaw, must walk away to die in privacy like a proud animal."

"Gray Foot has trouble walking but she still can ride; and you supply her in meat so she isn't going to starve while you or I are still alive. My grandfather was older than she is and your people killed him. Gray Foot is more a grandmother to me than she is to you. I will find her and bring her back."

Turning, she left to get Paint, leaving Peta standing with his mouth wide open. She mounted Paint and rode in a semicircle from the Canadian River around the camp. She made her circle wider every time. On her fourth pass she found tracks and saw they were heading for Antelope Hills. After Naduah entered the first canyon she had no trouble following Gray Foot's tracks. She found her sitting, singing her songs, while rocking back and forth.

Naduah put Gray Foot on Paint and started leading him back toward the camp.

"Please, leave me. I'm old and useless. I have lived a good life. I'm looking forward to going to my Happy Hunting Ground."

She took Gray Foot to Peta's tepee. With Sensa's help they got her off Paint and made her comfortable on a pallet. She and Sensa built a larger tepee by adding Gray Foot's poles and skins to Peta's tepee. She felt she now had more time, and could watch and care for her while she would cut up the meat. Naduah now made Peta feel more responsible for Gray Foot's care. While it wasn't the Comanche way, Peta had learned earlier that you can't win an argument with Naduah. She was Indian, but inside she was still white. Four days later Gray Foot was up helping Naduah cut meat to be dried when she saw two Comanche from Kotsatekas Comanche band riding hard through camp yelling, "The

Texas Rangers with Tonkawa Indians scouts attacked our camp and are now headed here!"

* * *

Iron Shirt and all the older men in camp picked up their war gear, mounted their ponies and headed out to defend their camp. The younger men were all out hunting buffalo. Iron Shirt, with his black painted face which stood for death, led his braves across the rolling plains straight for Rip Ford's Texas Rangers. As soon as the Rangers saw the Comanche coming, they stopped, cocked their rifles, and checked their Colts. Iron Shirt led his braves in a spinning circle, all the time screaming, yelling, and shrieking, trying to create their most powerful medicine upon the Rangers.

The Rangers watched calmly, spitting tobacco juice, waiting for the show to end. Iron Shirt withdrew his braves and for awhile the two groups just stared at each other. He was far in the lead, and moved closer to the Rangers. The braves stopped and watched as Iron Shirt with his old coat of Spanish armor rode forward. He was trying to show his great medicine to his braves. They had seen him do this many times. Five Sharps rifles fire as one; Iron Shirt fell from his horse and he was dead.

* * *

Peta and High Wolf heard the shots from the rifles. They both at the same time let out the Comanche yell and raced for their camp. The other braves followed them. As they came nearer to camp they heard shots farther off to the south. Turning towards the sound of the gun fire, they rode over a mound and saw the Rangers had started their attack. Peta began to ride straight for the Rangers. He saw Iron Shirt's horse standing and Iron Shirt lying on the ground. High Wolf grabbed him.

"Our arrows are no match for their guns. We will try to wear their horses out, staying out of their range. You go at them from the other side with half the braves. I will do the same on this side. Little Foot, you go and have the women bring the horse herd down into that ravine," he said as he pointed back over his shoulder.

* * *

High Wolf moved towards the Rangers. The Rangers turned to meet his charge. He turned and made a run for it. As soon as the Rangers turned, Peta led his group at the back of the Rangers. The

Indians were changing horses all the time. With fresh horses, they could out maneuver the Rangers tired horses.

* * *

The battle lasted for seven hours. The Rangers had made their presence felt. They had killed not only Iron Shirt, but seventy-five Kotsatekas Comanche. The Rangers also captured eighteen Comanche, mostly women and children, and also a herd of three hundred horses from Kotsatekas Comanche. The Rangers had two men killed and two men wounded.

* * *

High Wolf and Little Foot sat Iron Shirt on Peta's horse. Iron Shirt was lighter because the Rangers had taken his old coat of Spanish armor. Peta rode behind Iron Shirt, holding him upright as they rode through the camp. The people mourned the loss of their War Chief. They carried him into his tepee where his older men friends bathed and painted his face with vermilion. His eyes were sealed with red clay. Then they dressed him in his finest clothes and bent his knees up to his chest, with his head bent forward to the knees. With rawhide, they bound his legs and arms to his body in a secure position. They spread a large blanket on the ground. Iron Shirt was sat on it. After his natural warmth left his body the rawhide was removed. Then the People were permitted a final look at him.

Peta and the young braves were busy digging a deep hole on high ground. The other braves were busy gathering sticks and what few rocks they could find. When the grave was finished, Peta and the braves went into camp to view Iron Shirt. It was time for the burial. The blanket was folded around Iron Shirt and secured tightly with rawhide. The strongest braves picked Iron Shirt up and sat him on his horse. Sikway, Peta's mother, mounted the horse behind Iron Shirt, holding his body in position until they reached the burial site. The camp followed the body to its' final resting place, wailing and weeping.

Iron Shirt was placed in the grave sitting up, facing the rising sun. His saddle and bridle were taken off his horse and put in the grave with his ornaments, tobacco, pipe, knives, lance, shield, bow, and arrows. High Wolf killed Iron Shirt's horse close to the grave. All of these things Iron Shirt would need when he arrived in the Happy Hunting Ground, where all people are equal; but a warrior who died defending his people, got a special consideration.

Iron Shirt was then covered up with dirt which was packed around him. Then a layer of sticks were placed on top and filled with dirt. The grave was marked with rocks, buffalo skulls, and bones.

High Wolf made a speech for all the camp to hear. Peta had lost his father, but his bravery in the battle now made him a War Chief that any warrior would follow. Naduah was so proud of him. The People all started to take down their tepee because this camp was now a death camp. They would move on to a new camp. They wouldn't return to this site for two years. This would give time for all the bad spirits to leave the campground.

* * *

Naduah and Sensa took down and loaded their tepee. Gray Foot loaded all the bowls and small things. When they had finished, Naduah helped Gray Foot on her horse. Gray Foot sat on her horse straight and proud. She now had a new life with Naduah.

Chapter 24

PEASE RIVER ON MULE CREEK (Quanah) TEXAS.
NOVEMBER 1860

Peta Nocona's band had camped on the clear water of Mule Creek now for over a month. Naduah loved the campsite because it was the first place that Peta stopped after the attack on Fort Parker. It was here that she first met Gray Foot; how she missed her. She still felt sad when she thought of Gray Foot who had died a year ago. Naduah missed their companionship. Without it, she wasn't sure she would have made it in the Comanche way-of-life.

Gray Foot had always helped Naduah in past years with her children. Quanah, now nine years old, was practicing to become a warrior. Day after day he practiced picking up objects off the ground while his horse was running full out. Pecos was eight years old. He was old enough now to wear clothes, a breechcloth, leggings, and moccasins. Pecos rode his pony every day trying to become as one. She was proud of her two sons. Prairie Flower, still a baby and being her first girl, held a special place in her heart.

Peta and Sensa came into camp with three pack animals loaded down with buffalo meat. She helped Sensa unload the meat. She never noticed Peta enter the tepee until he came out with his face painted. He had painted a stripe of white underneath his eyes and below the white stripe his whole face was painted black, meaning death.

"Where are you going?" she asked.

"I am leading a raid back into Texas because Texans are easy picking. Their horses aren't protected."

"You have led three raids there already. How do you know they aren't waiting for you?"

"We will be in and out before they realize we are there," Peta said as he hurried away to get his horse.

* * *

Peta sat down outside his tepee and began drumming and singing his war songs. It wasn't long before you could hear drums being played and singing all over the camp. He stopped drumming and mounted his horse. The braves who were joining him on the raid fell in behind as they rode through the camp. He stopped at the edge of the campsite; there they all dismounted. He stood in the middle explaining where the raid would take place, and they all would come back with many horses. He mounted and rode to the west side of the camp with all of the braves following. The braves lined up according to their standing in the band. He led off the parade to signify that the party was leaving that night. He led the parade through the camp four times, as darkness fell on the camp.

A big fire had been built in the center of the camp. The spectators formed a circle around the fire leaving an opening for the dancers to enter. Only braves who were going on the raid could dance with their woman partner. The dance lasted until after midnight; then the braves said their good-byes and left.

Peta had no idea who he was raiding; all he knew was he was raiding the hated Texan. When the raiding party left Keechi Valley, they had captured over 500 horses, violated women, and killed 23 people. He didn't realize that this raid would take him close to Charles Goodnight's ranch in Black Springs Oran in Palo Pinto County.

* * *

One of Goodnight's neighbors rode in and told him of the Indian attack and they were heading west with a large horse herd. He spreads the word of the raid and asked for volunteers to go after the Indians. He started off in a northwesterly direction from Loving Valley following Peta's trail. It was raining hard. He followed Peta all the way to Pease River before heading back home.

When he arrived home, he found that seventy of his neighbors had volunteered under Jack Cureton's command and were at Fort Belknap. Captain Sul Ross commanded the Texas Rangers which numbered sixty, seventy settler volunteers, and a patrol from the 2nd Cavalry. Cureton appointed Goodnight as scout and guide. The army moved with Goodnight in the lead, followed by Ross' Rangers, Cureton's volunteers, and then the pack mules.

He led them in a northwesterly direction straight into the plains. He knew where he was going. It was the trail he had followed earlier that led to the Pease River. The weather had changed as it was raining when they left Fort Belknap. Now they were facing a Texas blue northern. The Rangers rode all day in the bitter cold and wrapped themselves in blankets and buffalo robes around the fire at night.

The Rangers arrived on the Pease River two weeks after Peta's raid in Keechi Valley. The next morning they moved over the sand hill toward Mule Creek. He was the first to see Peta's camp. Most of the Indians had left for a new campsite. The rest were packing getting ready to move. He started to signal Captain Ross, but Ross had already seen the camp.

* * *

Ross ordered the Rangers to charge the camp and shoot "anything that moves." The Rangers swept down on the camp yelling and shooting. Goodnight took aim at a small running form when her blanket slipped and he saw her blond hair.

"Don't shoot her! She's white', "Goodnight yelled.

The Rangers believed they had killed Peta, but instead they killed Chief No-bah who had tried to save the women and children. Peta wasn't in camp at the time. He and many of the braves were hunting buffalo. Sensa was wounded in the shoulder, but escaped with Naduah's sons, Quanah, and Pecos, in the tall grass near the river. The Rangers took Naduah and Topsannah to Camp Cooper.

* * *

Naduah was given to the Commander's wife to care for and guards were placed to see that she didn't escape. The first thing that Mrs. Evans did was give her a bath and dressed her in a dress. She hated the dress as it wasn't soft and loose fitting as her antelope dress. The people all talked in a strange tongue she couldn't understand. She wished she could get back to Peta and her sons. She had seen Sensa get shot but didn't know if she was dead or alive, it all happened so fast.

* * *

Everyone in Camp Cooper believed she was Cynthia Ann Parker. Captain Evans brought in Horace Jones, an Army interpreter, who talked to her. She remembered nothing of her past, only her Comanche life. She kept asking him about Peta and her sons. She could only talk some broken Spanish and Comanche. She hated the white people as they were her husband's enemies and they had taken her away from her family. For that, she could never forgive them.

* * *

Captain Evans sent a message to Isaac Parker stating they had captured a white girl and believed she was Cynthia Ann Parker. Isaac lived in Birdville on the main fork of the Trinity. He arrived the last week in January by wagon, accompanied by A. B. Mason and two of his neighbors on horseback. He had been told that if she was Cynthia Ann, he would have to guard her day and night.

Horace Jones was called again to talk to Naduah. This time Isaac asked the questions through Jones. He asked about certain events of her childhood before the Fort Parker attack. She just looked at them and never said one word. After over two hours of questioning, Parker said to Jones, "If this is my niece, her name is Cynthia Ann."

Before Jones could translate, the woman stood up and struck herself with her fist to her breast saying, "'Me, Cincee Ann'".

Isaac had Jones question her about other names of the Parkers. The only name she remembered was John, her brother's name. This satisfied Isaac because he knew John had been with the Comanche and had seen Cynthia Ann. Isaac put Cynthia Ann in a wagon.

* * *

Cynthia Ann had no way of knowing she would be confined to riding in the wagon for the next two weeks. She wished she were home and could ride Paint. The wagon was rough riding and the horses stirred up the dust. She had been in dust storms that were easier to breath in. Topsannah just slept and nursed, when she felt like it, as the ride didn't mean a thing to her.

She hoped when they stopped at night; somehow, she could escape. She realized they were traveling in an easterly direction which was taking her farther away from her Indian family. She had traveled many nights with Peta. She could use the stars to guide her back. The things that worried her, where would the band be and were Peta, Quanah, and Pecos still alive? When they camped at dark, she went over towards the brush to make her bed. Isaac came over and moved her back closer to the fire. She slept with one eye open, like a Comanche waiting for a chance to slip into the brush. All night long one of the men was guarding her so she never had a chance. When they arrived in Birdville, she and Topsannah were placed in a cabin that was hooked onto the main house by a breezeway. Cynthia Ann was locked in the house whenever one of family members weren't able to guard her. Twice she made good her escape and was brought back.

Chapter 25

The House of Representatives were discussing a bill that would give Cynthia Ann and Topsannah a new start in the White man's world. The bill was on the floor in the House. Mrs. Brown, Mrs. Raymond, and other friends of the family prepared Cynthia Ann for the trip to Austin. It was a social affair for the women, but not for her. She considered the way they dressed. It was very uncomfortable and the clothes restricted air movement. She wasn't use to being all wrapped up, but now she understood why the women fanned themselves all the time.

Arriving in Austin they entered the House of Representatives, but the congressmen scared her because she thought of them as chiefs. She had been told they were deliberating on her fate. She ran away like Peta had always told her to do when she was in danger. Mrs. Brown was able to catch her and guaranteed that the congressmen meant her no harm. They passed a bill granting Cynthia Ann a pension of one hundred dollars a year for five years beginning in 1861, and also gave her one league of land (three square miles).

Isaac was tired of worrying about her and asked her brother, Silas Parker Jr., to take her. Silas agreed and went to Birdville. Silas had ridden a horse and led a horse for her. This made her very happy. She ran and jumped on the horse carrying Topsannah. Silas lived on a farm north of Tailor. The first thing Cynthia Ann did after they arrived at the farm was lay Topsannah down on the ground and knelt beside her. She was convinced Topsannah's soul had been captured by demons of the white people. In front of her she smoothed a place on the ground and drew a circle and a cross. She kindled a fire on the cross, burned some tobacco, and then cut her breast to let her blood drip onto the flames. Lighting her pipe, she blew smoke toward the sun and meditated. She now believed Topsannah's soul was free.

* * *

Silas' wife, Mary, never adjusted to the ways of Cynthia Ann and Topsannah. She punished Topsannah whenever she had a chance and called her the 'Little Barbarian'. Cynthia Ann talked to her brother, Silas, about Mary's behavior and treatment of Topsannah. So he made arrangements with their sister, Orlena O'Quinn, who lived near Ben Wheeler.

* * *

Cynthia Ann and Topsannah were happy living with the O'Quinns. Orlena was teaching Topsannah to speak English. Later, however, Topsannah contacted a fever and died with influenza and pneumonia. Topsannah was five-years old. She now felt alone since she had heard Peta and Pecos also were dead. She asked Rufus O'Quinn if she could move to their sawmill located on the Neches River. They gave her permission and helped her move. Rufus looked in on her whenever he was in the area.

Her thoughts went back remembering the good times ... how she loved camping on the Pease River. It was there she met Gray Foot who was like a grandmother to her. She remembered all the things that Elder John had told her about God and heaven ... how God was always watching over us and when we die, we join him in heaven. If this was true then God must rule over the Happy Hunting Ground, from what Gray Foot had told her when she considered herself too old and useless. Now, she felt the same way as all her family and the people she loved were dead. She was no longer free to ride over the next hill. She felt she was a captive in the white man's world. She had made up her mind she would go to the Happy Hunting Ground where life continued on, braves still hunted, the women raised the children and took care of the meat and hides of the buffalo.

Everyday she took a walk along the river pretending she was back with the Comanche. As she came around the sawmill, she saw a man sitting in the shade. Before she could recognize him he yelled, "Come here, Naduah."

"Oh! Cohn Smith, you have come to take me back home to the Comanche," she answered as she gave him a hug.

"I can't take you back. If I did I would never be allowed back into Texas again. You are famous because the State of Texas has given you a pension and a land grant. Look at that old horse that I'm riding, it would never get us to the Arkansas River."

"I will get all the horses we will need. Just let me put my hands on a horse's mane and the horse is mine."

"But, Naduah, I just got myself married to a good woman. I can't leave her."

"Take me back. I will see that you get ten wives and ten horses. You have lived with the Comanche for years just like I did. You know that I speak straight."

"Since you were captured, things aren't the same. The Noconis band is no more. All the families have joined other bands. Peta, after you were captured, just disappeared."

After Cohn left, she just gave up. She went into mourning for Topsannah, Pecos, and Peta, like the Comanche she was. She cut her hair as short as possible, cut her breasts, rubbed tobacco into the wounds, and starved herself until she contacted influenza.

* * *

Rufus, busy with his spring work, missed seeing Cynthia Ann for over a week. He arrived at the sawmill at noon and noticed the front door shut. He knew Cynthia Ann never shut the door. He opened the door and there she lay on the floor dressed in her best pure white buckskin that she tanned herself. He knew she had gone to the Happy Hunting Ground she was always talking about.

Epilogue

Cynthia Ann died in 1870. Peta died in 1864 while picking plums on the Canadian River. Cynthia Ann was buried in the Foster Cemetery, south of Poyner, Texas. Cynthia Ann, if she had lived, would have been proud of her son, Quanah, who was the last Comanche Chief to surrender at Fort Sill in 1875. Major Mackenzie wrote a letter for Quanah to provide safe passage to Birdville to see his Uncle Isaac Parker. There he learned the "White Man's ways" and later was appointed Chief of Comanche by the government. He was good friends of President Theodore Roosevelt and made many trips to Washington.

Quanah tried to collect the money and land that the State of Texas promised Cynthia Ann. Charles Goodnight wrote many letters to his representative in Austin, but it was never given Quanah, in 1910, reburied his mother, Cynthia Ann, and Topsannah in the Post Oak Mission Cemetery near Cache, Oklahoma.

In 1957, the United States Government moved the bodies of Cynthia Ann, Topsannah, and Quanah to the military cemetery at Fort Sill. Cynthia Ann, even in death, had a conflict with her White world and her Indian world. At last her spirit can rest in peace lying between Quanah on her right and Topsannah on her left.

THE END